KILLIN' AMBUSH

The snow tapered off after a bit and the clouds broke to let the sun shine through on the plains. As I crested the hill, I saw my quarry: Sam Bonner and his hardcase pard. They were cresting the rise just ahead, within range of my Sharps. It was time to take them.

I threw a round in front of them just to make things interesting. They both whirled around, guns blasting. Sam's carbine slug kicked up some fresh powder about ten yards short of my mount. His pards shot wild, then set to scrambling down the hill out of sight.

Loading a fresh shell, I aimed careful and low and hit old Sam in the leg. He went down hard, rolling backward, but recovering right quick. He pumped another four rounds toward me, but was still shooting short. I raised my Sharps and had him in my sights, when I saw his arms go up. He was yelling something I couldn't understand, the wind being at my back. I put up my gun and moved closer.

"Drop it!" a man shouted behind me. It was Dutch Evarts, Bonner's pard, his Colt aimed straight at my head.

DEAD MAN'S HAND

RAY TOEPFER

ZEBRA BOOKS
KENSINGTON PUBLISHING CORP.

ZEBRA BOOKS

are published by

Kensington Publishing Corp.
475 Park Avenue South
New York, NY 10016

First printing: July, 1990

Printed in the United States of America

1

My pa was close to sixty when I was born, and the shock must have been too much for the poor old man, because he died shortly after. Ma made out pretty well, buying a boarding house with the money Pa left, and serving the best meals in Caliope, Kansas. For a while she raised me and my older half-brother Bill, until Bill up and went into business on his own, selling dry goods out of a store he'd set up cheap, and then selling real estate to folks who didn't know how much he'd paid for the land originally.

All of which is to say, by the time I was eighteen and Ma died of typhoid, Bill was 29 and had made his mark, and I was kind of left out of things. Well, not entirely. I always had a way with numbers, and Bill used me to figure out percentages and do lightning calculations, until I got smart and applied my talent to making money for myself.

My name's Charlie Pearse, but in some circles they call me Poker Pearse, because that's how I made my calculations work for me. I learned some from an old fellow named Stud Walker, who got his name from a preference for stud poker. He was the one who showed me that gambling is a kind of science, and that a good gambler always wins in an honest game. A good gambler knows the odds on any given hand, and he can figure them fast enough to know when the other fellow's hand is a loser before the other fellow even knows he's going to bet.

There's one hitch. It's nice to be quick with figures and good with the pasteboards, but you have to have an honest game, and back in the '70s an honest game was as hard to find as an honest congressman. Lacking an honest game, you had to learn to take care of yourself or figure on getting robbed. I don't like getting robbed any more than the next fellow, so I went shopping for a gun.

Lee Walker, he's the fellow was shot in '83 in El Paso in a fight over a dance-hall girl, told me to get a double-action Starr. In those days that was one of the few double-action revolvers around, and it was blessed with a big cylinder that could be converted to .44-40 metallic cartridges, which were a lot hotter than the .45 Colt or such-like. I learned how to shoot double-action at any range up to twenty yards. I could put six in a six-inch circle, and that's plenty good when you have a hardcase up against you. I never had to shoot anybody to prove how good I was; all I had to do was demonstrate on empty whiskey bottles behind any saloon in the town I happened to be in. I got a reputation without having to pay for it, you might say. In any game I figured was turning sour because of marked cards or green eyeshades or sleight-of-hand, all I had to do was put on my big country-boy grin, narrow my eyes, and announce that I was folding with my winnings. It always worked; they let me go without any fuss.

Well, not always. Sometimes I got an argument, and then I had to let my right hand drift close to the butt of the Starr before I could walk out.

Stud used to say, "Charlie, you can't solve everything with a gun. One of these days, somebody's going to call your bluff, and he's going to be faster on the draw and shoot straighter, and you're going to wind up in some godforsaken town's boot hill. And for what? Money is for fun and that's all there is to it."

One of these days came along. It was August 30, 1879, to be exact, and the godforsaken town was Denver, Colorado.

Now Denver had come up in the world ever since it had changed its name from Cherry Creek and become respectable. But there were still plenty of high-class whorehouses and saloons, and even more of them that were low-class. I'd drifted into town with fifteen hundred dollars to be invested in some high-class poker playing, and Deadwood and Cheyenne were off limits in my books. Deadwood was too rough and there was too much cattle money in Cheyenne for a man with only fifteen hundred to buck the system. That left Denver, and it was my bad luck to run into a gambling man known as Deadwood Sam Bonner.

Sam stood almost six foot and weighed about two-hundred, and his black hair and black handlebar mustache made him stand out in any crowd. He was sure to be the one the ladies picked, if they had a choice, but he was all man too, and he had the respect of other men in all things that took guts and a lack of the finer impulses.

I got in the game, and it didn't take me a whole long time to figure out that the cards were marked and that the saloonkeeper was in on the game. Sam

7

was cagey, though. He let me win a few hands, and by the end of an hour I was a couple of hundred ahead. I figured it was about time I quit and went on to greener pastures before Sam lowered the boom.

Now I never stood higher than five-foot-six, nor did I ever weigh more than one-thirty-five, and that gave a man like Sam a kind of advantage, you might say. But I got up and said I was through, banking hard on my country-boy grin and my reputation with the Starr to see me through.

Old Sam smiled. "That ain't friendly, Charlie. Seems like to me, you took my money and now you ain't going to give me a chance to win it back. Fair's fair, sonny."

I grinned some more. "It was a fair game, Sam, and I'm obliged to you for the fun. But I won what I won, and that's the way it is." I let my right hand come close to the butt of the Starr, where he could see I meant business.

But just about that time, a frontier Colt was peeping across the table at me out of Sam's big fist. I've never seen a man draw any faster than Deadwood Sam Bonner, and I hope I never do. It purely scared the hell out of me.

"Why don't you reconsider, Charlie? Set down and play a little more."

It was an order, no matter how you looked at it, and like Stud used to say, money is for fun. Death is kind of final. I sat down and Sam proceeded to win back his two hundred and five hundred more besides before he let me go. There's more ways than one a man can get an education, and I got an education that day. Don't ever try to bluff a man who's faster with a gun than you are, and make sure before you go into a game that the cards are clean and new.

I went outside and thought about the money I'd lost, and being a gambling man, the second thing I thought about was, How am I going to get it back?

2

I puzzled over that for three days, and then I solved the problem. If Sam was playing with marked decks, all I had to do was figure out how they were marked or else ask that the deck we played with be clipped. In those days cards were kind of high-priced, and when the edges got bent or frayed, the proprietor of the house would put the deck in a card trimmer and shave the edges.

Well, Sam lighted up like a Christmas tree when he saw me coming. The sucker was coming back for more. "Good to see you, Charlie. You coming back to get even?"

"Maybe. Thought I'd sit in whenever there's a vacant seat."

He nodded and turned his attention to separating two marks from their money. There were two other players, but I knew by now that they worked for Sam, so they didn't count. They always lost a little, just to make the game look right, but it was Sam's money they made and Sam's money they lost, so it didn't make any difference. If a mark complained, they'd tell him it was too bad, but they'd lost too, hadn't they? If he kept on complaining, Sam would show them his Colt, like he'd done to me, and that would end the argument.

About the time I had it figured out that Sam had

marked the aces with one dent and the kings with two, he gave a little signal to one of his shills, and I took a hand in the game.

He was a slick dealer, and he could deal from the bottom just as easy as most men can deal from the top. But I had an edge because I knew how his cards were marked. It took me fifty-five iron men and a little over an hour, and then I had the whole deck marked the same way. That was another little trick Stud had taught me. If a dealer marks certain cards, it's so he can pick them out of the rest of the deck. All you have to do is mark the rest of the deck the same way, and then the cards are all the same and he can't tell what he's doing. At least he can't until he catches on to what you've done, and gets himself a new deck that the saloonkeeper has marked in advance.

Sam didn't catch on until he started dealing himself what he thought were betting hands and found out he had nothing. But he still couldn't prove anything without admitting he'd been cheating all along. I was three hundred ahead of the game by that time, not counting the five hundred I'd lost three days before. If you counted that, I was into him for eight hundred dollars, and he didn't like that worth a damn.

"Let's have a new deck," he said, watching me.

I shrugged. "Up to you."

He was kind of surprised that I didn't kick up a fuss, but all I needed was an even break. When it came to playing poker without cheating, Sam was a babe in the woods. I was an expert.

I let him win a couple of hands with the new deck,

11

which was marked of course, and then I got the hand I wanted. I had three of a kind, ladies. Sam's partner opened, I checked, and the other two checked. Sam raised, which meant he probably had aces or kings. When it came to the draw, Sam took two cards, his partner took three and raised again, building the pot. I checked and waited to see what the other two had, and sure enough, one stayed and one folded.

Sam's two cards could mean he had bet on a pair, drawn nothing, and was bluffing. Or it could mean he'd bet on three of a kind, like me, and had improved his hand. I gave him a grin, picked up my two draw cards, and found myself with another winner, four ladies with an ace kicker. It was a good hand, but the question was, was it good enough to beat Sam's?

Sam could have a straight or a flush, but I guessed he'd dealt himself three kings or three aces and drawn nothing. Maybe a fourth ace or king? No, not an ace: I held one, so the most he could hold was a three-ace hand, and the odds were pretty much against that. Three or four kings? Maybe. There was only one way to find out.

"Well, sonny?" Forty talking to twenty-two. "You going to say something or just set there?"

"Tell you what, Sam," I said. "This is the last hand for me, win, lose, or draw."

He grinned. "Let's hear you say something worth listening to."

I nodded, pretending to be reluctant. "Raise you fifty."

There was a sort of hush around the table, as if everybody knew this one was between Sam and me.

12

At the end of it, somebody was going to get skunked or killed. I wasn't too worried; I had my back to the wall, so nobody could get behind me and signal to Sam or hit me over the head, and I had an ace in the hole nobody knew about.

"You're bluffing."

I shrugged. "Easy enough to find out, Sam."

"All right, I call."

I spread out the queens and the kicker. Sam stared at them for a long moment, and then he folded his cards. The other two marks pushed back their chairs and stood up. The one was a nervous city type, and he looked like he wanted no part of what was coming, but the other was a rancher I'd met a couple of days before, and he looked ready to back whatever play I wanted to make.

I stood up slowly, watching Sam's right hand while I pulled in the pot with my own. When Sam's hand trembled a little, as if it was making up its mind to go for the Colt, I pointed with my left hand and said, "Sam? Don't."

His eyes fastened on my sleeve and I purely enjoyed the look of surprise that came over his face as he saw my other ace in the hole. I'd strapped a derringer to my left forearm, and I could fire both barrels with a string looped around my neck. All I had to do was straighten my arm, and Sam's poker days were over for good.

"Take it," he said thickly. "I'll get it back one of these days, though."

About that time the city man made tracks as if he'd suddenly found pressing business elsewhere.

My new friend, the rancher, backed off a little to

cover the operation while I counted out my chips in front of Sam. I'd taken him for a little under a thousand dollars, and all of it won fair and square. He reached in his pocket very slowly and came up with a wad of greenbacks and counted it out for me.

"One of these days you're going to turn around, sonny, and I'll be there. That's a promise."

"If that's the way you want it, Sam," I told him, "I'll be ready for you."

I stuffed the money in my pocket, and then the rancher cashed in his chips and we moved backward to the door. All very neat, no violence, no gunplay. Just neat.

"Thanks a hell of a lot, partner," I told the rancher.

"Don't mention it. I liked the way you took that bastard. He was cheating, wasn't he?"

I nodded. "He marked aces and kings."

"How'd you beat that?"

"I marked all the other cards the same way."

He laughed. "Oh, hell, come on and have a drink with me. Maybe you can teach me something about poker I don't know."

"No game," I said immediately. "I'm about pokered out."

He shook his head. "I ain't trying to get your money, sport. I'm just the curious kind."

We found a high-class bar about five streets over, and I explained the finer points of playing poker for profit. It's not that simple, but it's not that hard to learn either. What you have to do is figure the odds of your drawing the hand you want, and then you have to figure the odds of betting on it. Like, if you hold a pair of aces, there's only two more in the

14

deck. In a five-card draw game with five players, there's twenty-five cards already out, leaving twenty-seven. Your chances of drawing another ace are one in twenty-seven, because somebody else has an even chance of holding one already. If you don't draw it, then it's a good idea to listen close to the betting and fold the minute somebody sounds like he's got something, because he probably does.

There's never any sense to throwing good money after bad, and the odds are on somebody's going to be able to beat your aces. It is not that great a hand, and that is a fact.

On the other hand, sometimes it's smart to bet your aces and lose, just to make the others think you're not so smart. Then when you've got a flush or four of a kind, you can bet and raise, and they'll stick with you, because they think you're a damn fool or bluffing, one, and you can rake in some good pots later in the game.

"Name's Jim Thatcher, by the way," the rancher said. "You ever want to come around and work on a ranch, come up and see me."

"I'm Charlie Pearse."

"Might have known," he grinned. "You're the one they call Poker Pearse."

"I've been called that," I said modestly.

"Well, I've got a spread up near Julesberg. If you get around that way, look me up."

"Yessir, I might just do that."

"For now, it might be a good idea if you kissed Denver City goodbye." He finished his drink and set down the glass. "I don't think that sonofabitch was kidding when he said he was coming after you."

15

"No more do I."

"Well, no offense meant, but you're never going to take him with a gun. He's a fast man even in a fair fight, and if he has it his way, it ain't going to be a fair fight."

"I know that, Mr. Thatcher."

"Jim. Let's get the hell out of here."

3

Jim Thatcher and I parted company a couple of blocks down the street. He went to his hotel, and I headed for my hotel room.

But on the way I got to thinking. There was nothing in that room that particularly interested me except the little valise with my clean clothes. You can always buy more clothes, but you can't buy back your life. The odds were on that Deadwood Sam Bonner knew all about me and about that room, and that his two shootists were already out looking for me and for the three thousand iron men I'd won off Sam. One thing you could count on with Sam was that when it came to gunplay he was no bluffer.

I figured the odds. I could go down to the depot and take a train for someplace. I could buy a horse at the livery stable and ride out. Or I could hang around the railroad yards and catch me an empty boxcar.

The first choice was out, because that's what Sam would expect me to do. Buying a horse wasn't too bright either, because Sam might figure I'd be too smart to take a train. But a boxcar might do the trick. Once I got aboard, there was no way he could catch me or even trace me.

Good, that was settled. The next thing to think of was where I was headed. That was easy when I got

17

down to it. I'd go home, back to Caliope, Kansas, where I grew up. Not too many people in Denver knew Caliope even existed, let alone that I'd come from there, and if I hitched a ride on a freight train as far as Wallace, I could buy a horse and disappear for a time. Ride up to Caliope and visit my good old half-brother, Bill.

I ran into a tall, skinny, and obliging drunk in an alley and gave him my coat and hat. They were give-aways, because Sam's shootists would be looking for a medium-sized fellow with a black Prince Albert coat and a black, flat-crowned hat. I didn't worry about them shooting the drunk: he had a good six inches on me, and a blind man could have seen the difference.

I took the derringer off my arm and stuck it in the top of my right boot, hitched the Starr around to where I could reach it comfortably, and started walking for the railroad yards.

I gave the depot a wide berth and found a train made up with empty boxcars and coaches full of people headed back east. When nobody was looking, I snuck into one of the boxcars and made sure it was empty. Then I peeked around the corner of the door and watched the depot. Sure enough, after maybe five minutes, one of the shootists came nosing out of the depot toward the coaches. He got on the front one and walked his way through to the rear one. He was a stocky sort of fellow with almost yellow hair. Sam Bonner had called him Dutch.

About that time Sam came out of the depot and whistled to the yellow-haired fellow. He went over to Sam and they stood talking for a couple of minutes. I guessed they were wondering whether to hang around and maybe go through the boxcars, or go look elsewhere. I'd seen passengers getting on the coaches, so I guessed it wouldn't be too long before we got started. The same thought must have occurred to Sam, because the two of them came sauntering over toward the first boxcar in line, five ahead of me.

If you've ever tried to hide in an empty boxcar, you know it's impossible. You can't hang from the roof, and even if you get up on top the brakeman's going to spot you and kick you off. It's kind of a no-win situation. To make matters worse, old Sam was smart enough to lend a hand himself, so I couldn't duck out while his partner was searching another car.

I risked a peek and saw the stocky man's butt going up into the car next to mine. Sam was nowhere in sight, which had to mean he was covering the opposite side of the train by now. The third man, a sort of skinny fellow with red hair, would be checking out livery stables.

Feet tramped down the roof of the car next to mine and paused. I heard a squealing, rasping sound, and then the feet came down the roof of my car and paused again. A voice bellowed, "Get the hell out of that boxcar, bum!" and I knew the brakeman had been turning the brake wheels to free the brakes on the cars and had spotted Sam and his partner.

"Looking for a killer," Sam said in that pleasant voice of his. "We're deputies."

"Let's see a badge, fellow."

I guessed that Sam would have a piece of tin on him for emergencies like this. A lot of crooks had them. But I never found out, because about that time another voice yelled, "Bo-a-rd!", and the brakeman scrambled over the caboose and released the last of the brakes. All I had to do was hope the train moved out before the shootist came to my car.

It didn't happen. Like drawing to an inside straight, the odds were against me. There was plenty of time to look in the last car, and they weren't going to pass it up, brakeman or no.

Somebody was going to stick his head in that door inside of the next minute or two; that much was certain. I made an educated guess: that somebody would probably be right-handed, and if he was, he was going to look to his left first. And that did happen.

The south door was closed, so Sam would have to open it to see inside. I let the yellow-haired man get his head in for a peek to the left, and when he turned his head to the right, I had the Starr right down where he could see it without any trouble, it being about two feet from his head and looking him in the right eye.

"Get in here," I told him quietly. "And don't make a sound."

He thought about it for a split-second, and then the Starr convinced him and he scrambled up. I motioned him over in a corner and as he started for it, the train gave a couple of bucks and jerks and began to move. Panic came over his face and he looked longingly at the door. "Forget it," I told him. "You're going for a train ride."

"Hey, you got it wrong!" he pleaded, and he turned toward me.

"Face the other way," I said.

The train chuffed its way past the shacks on the outskirts of Denver and kept up a brisk pace, probably twenty-five or thirty miles an hour, through the long, flat prairie. I waited until I figured we were ten or fifteen miles out in the middle of nowhere, and then I pointed to the door and told him to jump.

"I'll break a leg!" he complained.

"For a fellow who was ready to turn me over to Sam, it seems to me you're mighty particular."

"I wouldn't have turned you over to Sam!"

"Git!" I told him. "I can shoot you first, if you'd rather."

He gave me a last accusing look, and then he jumped through the door and went tumbling over and over down the embankment.

There was one other matter of business I had to take care of. I fished around in the money I'd won from Sam until I found a ten-dollar bill, and I tucked it in my shirt pocket until the train stopped for water, which was maybe forty miles east of Denver. I stood in the door and waited until the brakeman came along to test the wheels and look for hot-boxes, and then I showed him the ten-dollar bill and told him I'd be obliged if I could ride east as far as the cars went.

"You could ride up front in a coach for that kind of money," he said suspiciously.

"I could, but I like this better."

"Why d'you want to ride in a boxcar?"

"I got my reasons," I grinned, and I let him see the butt of the Starr. I held the money where he could take it, and he had a mighty wrestle with his conscience, maybe for half a second, and then he took it.

After we got started again, I pulled off my boots and made a kind of pillow and went to sleep. There was nothing else to do until we got to someplace big enough to boast a livery stable and a clothes emporium, and that meant Wallace, Kansas.

4

When I woke up, it was dusk and the train had stopped at a station. That in itself didn't mean much, because there was a little station for water every ten miles or so, but this one looked big enough to be Wallace. I put on my boots and went to the door of the car, where the cool air of evening hovered like a promise of better things to come.

The train would stop here for the night, I guessed. Although there were few buffalo now, there was always the chance of an Indian ambush. I looked through the gloom and finally made out the lights of the Wallace House. I considered going in and ordering a meal, but only briefly. My clothes were filthy from lying in the boxcar, and in addition I had to leave as little sign of my passage as possible. Sam's yellow-haired shootist would be back in Denver by now, even walking, and Sam would learn I'd been on the train. His next move would be to check every station along the line to find out where I'd left the train. My next move would be to break trail, and this was the best place to do it.

I walked up the street to Robidoux's store, where it was said you could buy anything from a Sharps rifle to a new suit. There were things I needed before I went anywhere, and I had to take the chance of buying them and hoping Sam wouldn't pick up my trail

23

until I was safely gone. I guessed I had maybe twelve hours before the next east-bound train came in.

The store was open, lighted by flaring kerosene lamps, and it had a good smell of food, of rattrap cheese and freshly ground coffee, of good cloth and leather and well-worn wooden floors. I helped myself to water from a big tin cooler with a cup chained to it, and then I found a clerk and asked him about buffalo hunting south of Dodge City.

"Pretty near played out," he said. "You should have come in three or four years ago. You might find some down in Texas though."

I shrugged as if it were a matter of indifference to me. "I'll try my luck."

He took my order for crackers and cheese, salt and flour, coffee and cigars, and then I asked to see a rifle. "You'll be wanting a Winchester?" he asked.

"For buffalo?" I grinned.

He shrugged as if it didn't matter to him, but I could see what he was thinking. A new Winchester would sell for twice what a Sharps would bring. Nobody wanted the big buffalo guns any more. "I got a nice Sharps," he said grudgingly. "Used, but nice. I can throw in a reloading kit with it."

The Sharps was worn, but the bore was clean and the lands were sharp and clear. It had a folding tang sight, and the caliber was .50-110, which was plenty of gun for buffalo, elephants, and small locomotives.

I added the Sharps and the reloading kit and two boxes of shells to my other purchases and told the clerk to hold them while I went looking for a horse. He gave me a grin of faintly disguised contempt, as if to say that all hide hunters were alike: dirty, disreputable, and generally broke. But he directed me to a

24

stable where he said I could find a passable horse and gear.

There was no sense in rushing things. I wanted Sam to follow my trail to Wallace, and I wanted him to think I believed he'd talk to the clerk and the hostler and decide I'd gone to Texas. He wouldn't buy that story, of course; he was too smart for that. But it would point his head south, and he'd figure me to go to the Indian Nations and drift east, maybe to Arkansas or up to Missouri. By the time he found out he was wrong, my trail would be too cold to follow, and that was the way I wanted it.

Very few people in this world really want to kill anybody. I was no exception. I wasn't going to make Sam Bonner a present of the money I'd won from him, but I didn't want to have to try to kill him to keep it, either. He'd have to try to kill me before I'd raise a hand against him.

That night I headed out of Wallace, south, on the Dodge City trail. I followed it for maybe ten miles, and then I got off the trail and worked my way around the fort and the city until I came out five miles north of town around midnight, and I made camp near the north fork of the Smoky Hill River. The trick now would be to stay out of sight until I reached Caliope, sixty miles to the northeast.

I built a small fire and made coffee and ate some of the crackers and cheese, and then I put the fire out and lay back with my head on my new hat and watched the shooting stars and wondered what kind of reception I'd get in Caliope.

When I'd left, five years before, most of the town had been at least neutral, if not friendly. There were people who liked me, who took my part. There was also Pete Moffatt, and unless Pete had had a miraculous change of heart, he would try to kill me if I came back. You could say I was caught between the rock and the hard place. On the one hand I had Sam chasing me and the money, and on the other I had Pete Moffatt. But from where I sat in camp that night, Pete looked like a better choice than Sam.

It had started with Pete's daughter, Sara. She was a pretty enough girl, but I had eyes only for Mary Lou Barnes, the daughter of the local preacher. Mary Lou was quite a lady, and she was always after me to make something of myself, whatever that meant. We never got as far as talking about getting hitched or anything like that, but I could tell that was what she had in mind. And just about the time I had made up my mind to quit going off on hunting parties and playing a little friendly poker in the Emporium saloon, and buckling down to hard work for my halfbrother Bill so I could make something of myself, as Mary Lou put it, the roof fell in.

Sara Moffatt was in the family way, and she named me as the father. That was pure hogwash, and I told Pete Moffatt so to his face. I told Bill too, but Bill put on a sad face and said I'd better own up to my wild oats and do the right thing by Sara. Pete came to town with Sara and two of his riders and a meanlooking double-barreled scattergun, and I found myself standing with Sara in front of Parson Barnes saying "I do" like I meant it.

Sara and I set up housekeeping in a one-room shack on the edge of town, and it was a mistake from the word Go. I tried to tell her it wasn't so bad, that we could probably make a go of things if we worked at it, but the more I accepted the bad hand I'd been dealt, the more she cried and moped. I never asked her who the father was, and she didn't tell me.

Bill gave me a better job in the store he'd started, and he told me he was proud that I'd done my duty by Sara, even if I'd needed some prodding to do it. He even said in a rash moment that some day he might just let me buy the store for the cost of the goods in it. I didn't believe him, but it sounded nice just the same. Pete Moffatt had no use for me, but sometimes he'd stop by and see Sara when I was at the store. I always knew, because she was in a worse state after his visits.

It might have gone on like that forever, with me tending the store and her tending her misery, but one day I came home and found her sobbing as if her heart would break. "I can't go on like this, Charlie," she said. "I lied about you, and it's killing me."

"I know that," I told her. "But it don't matter now. What does matter is making a good home for that little one. Some day we're going to look back on this and kind of laugh at all the hoops we made ourselves jump through."

"I don't love you," she said.

"I know that, but it's not the only thing in this world. We can still like each other."

"I still love him," she said, and I didn't have to ask who she meant. "He let me down."

"And to protect him, you named me." I finished it for her.

"I'd have done anything for him."

Looking back, I can see where Sara was always a little simple. That was probably how she got in the mess she did, and her carrying on about it was an indication of how simple she was. Instead of putting

27

it behind her and trying to make a family and stay friends with me, she lived back there in the past with her lover, whoever he was, and she had no thought for the present and even less for the future.

It could have gone on that way forever, I suppose, but one day I came home from the store and found her dead. She'd drunk two bottles of laudanum, which is tincture of opium and can kill you just as well as a number of other things, like lye or .44 revolvers or a coil of rope or too much whiskey.

I sat there and bawled my eyes out, out of pity for her and out of sorrow for her child whom she'd killed too. But that was the way with Sara; she could only think of one thing at a time, and generally that was herself.

The funeral was the next day, and at first the Reverend Barnes didn't want to say anything over the grave, but I went to him and did some preaching of my own, about forgiveness and Christian charity, and it didn't take him too long to see things my way. We went out to the graveyard and the sun beat down like a club while the preacher said what he had to say, and then they started filling in the grave and I turned to go.

But Pete Moffatt had his own axe to grind, and he ground it good. He caught me unawares and fetched me a lick to the jaw that might have broken it, if he hadn't been in too much of a hurry. Even so, he managed to beat the hell out of me, claiming I'd either killed Sara myself or driven her to kill herself. When he was done and I was a pulp, he told me the next time he saw me he was going to kill me.

Bill took me to Doc Meyer, who patched me up pretty well with sticking plaster, whiskey, and some

28

kind of pills, and I slept around the clock.

When I woke up, Bill gave me two hundred dollars and a horse and told me not to think of hanging around to find out if Pete would keep his word. "My advice is to ride far and fast and don't come back," he told me, and at the time it seemed like pretty good advice. People like Pete Moffatt can't be reasoned with, and I was too green then to know that you never run away from your troubles. You can only carry them with you, like any other useless baggage.

5

That's what I thought about that night out there on the prairie, and I thought too that it was time to ride back to Caliope and get the record straightened out. I was going back to find a place to lay low until Deadwood Sam Bonner gave up and quit looking for me, but I was also going back to convince Pete Moffatt that I'd had nothing to do with Sara's getting in the family way or with her killing herself.

I didn't know if I'd succeed at either one, but I was sure as hell going to try.

That part of the country wasn't settled, and it wasn't likely to be for a few years to come. The Indians had come through the year before, as I'd read in the Denver newspaper, and they'd killed a bunch of settlers up north, along the Solomon River. It kind of put a damper on things, and I guess I wouldn't have too much trouble staying away from people until I got to Caliope.

I rode through the next day, making the best time I could, and I got to Caliope around sunset. Both the horse and I were wore to a frazzle, and I could imagine we looked like a couple of bums. It was kind of funny when I thought about it, because I had almost three thousand dollars in my ragged pockets. But the way the town treated me was going to dictate how I spent my money.

Caliope hadn't changed a whole lot. Sol Levitan still had his general store in the middle of the main drag, a couple of blocks west of Bill's store, where I'd worked until the day of Sara's funeral. Jim Hagen's Emporium saloon was doing business at the old stand, although he'd put in a new set of swinging doors, real batwings like the fancy drinking places in Denver and Cheyenne. The church had a new coat of white paint, and there was a new feed shed alongside the livery stable. That was about the only new building in town, except for a neat little mail-order house set back a hundred feet from the main drag.

I hitched my horse in front of Bill's grocery store and went in. A kid I didn't know was tending the cash register, and he made a point of showing me the stock of a sawed-off scattergun right beside it, just in case I had ideas of robbing the till. I asked after Bill, and the kid told me Mr. Pearse was home for the evening.

"Down at Mrs. Durning's?"

"No. At his house. The new one down there. Come all the way from Chicago, it did."

"When did that happen?"

"A year ago, when he got married." He looked at me suspiciously. "You want to leave your name, mister, I'll tell him in the morning."

"That's all right. I'll just ride on down there and see him now."

He looked at me as if I'd just announced my intention to pay a social call on God. "I don't think he'd like that, mister. If you was to stop by in the morning, here at the store, you could see him then."

"Sure," I said, and then I went ahead and did what I'd intended to do all along.

It was a nice little house with a lot of gingerbread decoration under the gables and all along the porch, and somebody had planted hollyhocks right next to the railing where they'd look pretty. There was a pretty little cottonwood tree set where it could shade the house from the worst of the morning sun, and in maybe five years it would be big enough to do the job it had been planted to do.

I hung the reins of the horse over the gate post and went up the walk, conscious all along of the contrast between my ragged clothes and the clean white paint of the house, and the farther I walked the more I thought it would have been smarter to get some new clothes from Sol Levitan before I made an appearance. And then I thought, hell, this is my pretty-near brother I'm calling on.

The woman who opened the door looked familiar, and it didn't take me but a minute to recognize Mary Lou Barnes. It took me only a little longer to figure out what she was doing here: she lived here, she was Bill's wife.

"Why—Charlie! What in the world are you doing here?"

"I thought I'd stop by and see Bill. Didn't know you two were married."

"Last year," she said with a little smirk of satisfaction. "Bill's inside resting."

At that point Bill came out of the parlor. He looked well-scrubbed and prosperous, which meant he had on a clean white shirt and his boots were shined up like a couple of mirrors, and he sported the beginning of a paunch. Life had treated old Bill pretty well, and I wondered how much of that was due to the grocery store and how much was due to his real estate speculations.

"Charlie, it's good to see you," he said, but he looked as if I was something the cat had drug home when nobody was looking. "You need money?"

"I'm comfortably fixed, Bill."

"Just on your way through?"

"I figured on hanging around for a while," I told him, just to set the record straight.

He exchanged glances with Mary Lou, and apparently she told him No, because he said that maybe I could drop around by the store in the morning and we could talk about things.

I grinned and said I might do that, but he'd probably run into me around town, and then I turned and walked away. I wasn't going to be invited into their new mail-order house any more than I was going to be asked to come into the grocery business as a partner. And that was all right with me. When I'd worked for Bill before, I'd done all the donkey work and he'd made all the money. Then I had to take it, because I didn't know any better and because I needed the money. But now I didn't own a thing except a horse, a saddle, a couple of guns, and three thousand dollars, and I liked it that way. Any time I wanted to move along, I could, and I didn't have to ask anybody's permission to do it.

I put the horse up at the livery stable and headed down to Purdy's barber shop for a bath and a shave and haircut, and when I finished there it was dark out and the lights from Sol Levitan's clothing store and Jim Hagen's saloon spilled out across the boardwalk into the street.

Sol, at least, was glad to see me. "By golly, you have grown, Charlie! Two inches and twenty pounds, yah?"

"Just about that, Sol. How've you been keeping yourself?"

"Pretty good, Charlie. We're going to be the county seat one of these days, and then Caliope is going to boom."

"Got plans?"

"A couple of lots. That's better than plans."

I nodded agreement. "I hope you make money on them, Sol. Now do you think you've got some clothes would fit me?"

Sol had come to Caliope ten years before, hauling a wagon-load of dry goods and high hopes along with him. He was a good merchant, by which I mean he made a profit without cheating, which was more than I could say for some of the merchants in Caliope, not to name any names. He had two strikes against him: he was an outsider and he was a Jew. But in ten years nobody seemed to remember either. His good business practices had made him a good man to deal with, fair and even lenient, and his willingness to talk with anyone, anytime, had established him as a good person to know.

He took measurements and came up with a black broadcloth suit that looked like the one I'd had to leave behind in Denver. I got a couple of white shirts to go with it, and then I bought some trail clothes, levis and a couple of checked shirts, and a good pair of Justin boots I could wear with the suit. Sol let me change behind a curtain in the back. I bundled my rags and asked Sol to take care of throwing them away, and then I wore the trail clothes out the door. Sol promised to take in the suit and have it ready for me the next day. I left him the better part of fifty dollars to cover the whole deal, but what the hell? I could afford to be a big spender now I'd shaken Sam Bonner.

I hadn't found out too much about the town from Purdy, who was more interested in getting rid of me than in gossiping, so I went into Jim Hagen's Emporium saloon.

Like Sol, Jim was friendly, but reserved. I bought drinks for him and for me, and then I ordered a schooner of beer and asked him about the chances of getting something to eat.

"Sure. Martha can fix you up some eggs and side meat and biscuits. Will that do it?"

"Hell, yes. I'm hungry enough to eat the north end of a south-bound skunk without salt."

He grinned and went into the back room for a moment.

Jim Hagen had been in Caliope ever since I could remember, which was pretty near as long as there'd been a town. He habitually wore plaid trousers, a white shirt, and high-top button shoes. I'd never known him to wear anything else. He was stocky without being fat, and he moved quickly on his feet, almost like a dancer. Once he told me he was half-Irish, half-German, but that was about all I knew about him. His wife, Martha, was as pleasant a person as you'd want to meet, always friendly and smiling, and if she knew anything sinister about her husband's background, you couldn't tell it from the way she acted.

Only once did Jim let something slip. Not anything he said — he was too cagey for that — but the way he handled a young tough who had grandiose ideas. The kid had come in looking for trouble, trying to pick a fight, and Jim politely invited him to leave. He wouldn't, of course: it was part of his act. "Make me," he said, and he kept his hand close to the butt of his gun.

Jim came around to the front of the bar, facing the kid, and when he was ready he dared the kid to draw. "Go ahead. Show me how tough you are," he said.

The rest of us watched to see what Jim would do if the kid threw down on him. We didn't have long to wait. The kid went for his gun and Jim knocked his right arm sideways with his left hand and hit him in the gut with his right. As the kid doubled up, Jim got his gun and laid the barrel alongside his head.

"Knew a fellow like him once," Jim said. "Down in Mobeetie, Texas, it was."

"How long did you know him?" somebody asked.

Jim's eyes turned flat and cold, and suddenly it wasn't a funny question any more. "About five minutes," he said, and every one of us knew that there were things in Jim's past that didn't bear raking up.

When he came back from talking to Martha, I noticed that he'd put on a little weight. Nothing to worry about, nothing to slow him down, but a couple of pounds here, a couple there. Life was treating him right, the way it looked.

"Martha'll fix you up something. What've you been up to?"

"One thing and another. Playing a little poker, mainly."

He snapped his fingers. "I should have made the connection. You must be Poker Pearse, right?"

I modestly acknowledged the fact.

"Well, Charlie. Your reputation's come up here. Fellow came by a couple of months back and told me he played with you up at Platte Bridge. Said you never cheated that he could see, but you won some mighty good pots off him."

"Don't have to cheat to win, Jim. All you have to do is play good poker."

He looked past me at the door, but nothing moved outside. "You planning to hang around here a while, Charlie?"

"For a while, yes."

"There's something you ought to know. Pete Moffatt's still got an eye out for you. Every time he gets liquored up, he says he's going to kill you."

"Drunk talk don't bother me a whole lot, Jim. If he wants a fight, I'm in pretty good shape to take him on. I'm not a kid any more."

Jim reached for his towel and started polishing a glass, and then Martha came in from the kitchen with a plate of eggs, another of side meat, and still a third of biscuits. She set them down at a table in back and smiled a greeting before she went back to the kitchen.

I didn't need a second invitation to get into the food, and I washed it down with three cups of the blackest, hottest coffee I'd had in days.

Two men came in arguing about whether President Hayes would run for a second term. Jim served them, and then a drifter came in. He looked something like what I'd looked like an hour ago, and he sipped steadily at a beer and checked out the room in the mirror over the bar.

Jim came over and carried my plates back to the kitchen, and then he came over and sat down at the table with me, bringing us a couple of beers in case we got thirsty. I took it as an invitation to talk, and that is what it was. Only I got Jim to do the talking.

Bill had done all right for himself, Jim said. He'd taken the money he inherited from our dad and invested whatever was left, after buying the store, in lots. There was good money to be made there, Jim said, if Caliope got to be the county seat. "You found out he got married, I guess?"

I nodded. "Mary Lou Barnes. I've already had the honor."

"As I remember, you was kind of sweet on her at one time yourself."

"You could put it that way."

He looked at me gravely. "You can count your blessings and thank old Bill for doing you a favor."

"How's that?"

"She runs his ass around the lot every day of the week and twice on Sunday. Old Bill does just like she says, and I want to tell you, she keeps him on a mighty tight rein. Way I hear it, he's got to take off his shoes when he comes in the house, so he don't get her pretty new floor dirty. And she comes down to the store a couple times a day to make sure he ain't making sheep's eyes at any other woman."

"It wouldn't have happened to me."

He chuckled. "Don't be too sure. When a woman sets out to run a man's life for him, she can generally manage the job. You might have been just as unlucky as he was."

"Could be."

"I know it. There's some other things about this town you ought to know. Bill has been growing some, ever since Mary Lou roped him in. He's got his finger in a lot of pies, owns a piece of pretty near every store in town. I would say she's the brains behind the push. Now, about the only two places I know that he don't have a piece of are this one and Sol Levitan's store. Sol is naturally a cagey fellow, and he's got too much sense to let anybody shove him out. And that's where Sol and me see eye to eye. I had a chance two-three years ago to mortgage this place and buy me a lot and house on the edge of town. Well, Martha wanted that more'n anything else. But I said no. You borrow money from the bank, it's like borrowing it from Bill, because he owns half the bank too. And he charges ten percent compound. No way a fellow could pay that off in twenty years."

In those days, four percent was considered about the tops for a loan, so it seemed to me Bill was doing a little gouging.

"What's he trying to do? Buy out the town?"

Jim nodded. "That's about the size of it. I talked it over with Sol, and he figured Bill wants to lend money so he can foreclose and take it all. If Caliope gets to be county seat, he's going to make a fortune out of it, because he'll own land and lots and stores and the whole kit and caboodle. Now even if it doesn't, he's still a prosperous man, you might say, even by Barnes standards. The old preacher ain't no slouch when it comes to making a buck."

"Seems like it ought to be fun to hang around and see what happens."

"You could put it that way," Jim said. "On the other hand, Bill might just not like the idea of a half-brother with no visible means of support hanging around Caliope. It might be bad for his reputation. Besides, he'd have to waste time worrying about what you were going to do next."

"I don't get that part about reputation."

"Well, folks might think he was helping you out, and that wouldn't square with his hard-nosed attitude, which he has been taking pains to develop over the years."

Business started to pick up after that, and Jim went back behind the bar. A few cowhands drifted in to do a little mild drinking, and after a while some of them sat down at a table with a bottle of red-eye and called for cards. I watched them play for a little while, and then I told Jim I'd better find me a place to sleep. He nodded and said Mrs. Durning still kept a pretty good boarding house, if I was planning to hang around for a while.

"I don't know how long I'll be staying," I told him.

"Well," he said. "You come around tomorrow morning, not too early, and we'll have a little talk: I've got an idea you might be interested in. If you're not, no hard feelings. Fair enough?"

"Fair enough," I told him, and I picked up my Sharps and my saddlebags and walked down the street to Mrs. Durning's boarding house, which had once belonged to my mother.

If there was anybody in Caliope who was apt to stand by me in case of need, it was Jim Hagen. Like I said, Jim went back pretty near to the beginning of the town, and when things were hard, he stuck up for me. There were times when I worked at Bill's store that I would wonder what the sense to it all was. I was working as hard as I could, getting nowhere, and constantly taking abuse from Bill and his head clerk. When things got particularly rough, I went to Jim.

It had started with a Sunday when there was nothing to do but sit in my room in the boarding house and read uplifting books. That generally meant the Bible or evangelical tracts with titles like "Sinner Be Saved!" and "Our Heavenly Home." Now, I had nothing against being saved, and a ten-year-old boy hasn't the experience to argue with Our Heavenly Home. In fact, there were a lot of days when it seemed to me that Our Heavenly Home had to be a lot better than the one I was in.

That Sunday I walked home from church with my mother and watched the leaves falling from the tree in our front yard and thought about the wide prairie beyond the town and the wonderful adventures that lay just out of reach. But of course there was Sunday reading to do and chores, and besides I had never been out of sight of town. To put it bluntly, I was more than a little scared. Scared of my mother and scared too of what I'd find out there in the long swells of land.

There's a time when you have to fish or cut bait though, and I went up to my room, put on my every-day clothes, and skinned out the window to the big elm tree in the backyard and from there to the ground. That was half the battle won.

I got out the back gate and headed north for the long ridge that shut off the town from the prairie beyond, and when I reached it, it was as if I were standing on the dividing line between two countries. On the one hand, there was Caliope, raw and new and only partly finished. On the other, there was the vast and mysterious prairie. In those days, there were still buffalo in the land, buffalo and antelope and deer. When you've got deer, of course, you've also got coyotes and wolves. And every so often, you'd come to a prairie-dog village. You could see hawks and rattlesnakes, and maybe even Indians.

It was scary, but it was exciting too.

At first I stayed close to the ridge. I walked behind it, only climbing back every so often to look at the town and make sure it was still there. But after a while I got bolder, and I walked out onto the prairie, scaring the dogs back into their holes, kicking at the tall grass, and even going up and over some of the little hills that broke up the flat monotony.

The sun was low in the sky before I thought about turning back. It came as something of a surprise to discover that I didn't know which way to turn. I hadn't kept track of where I'd wandered, and when I thought I'd reached the ridge from where I could see Caliope, I hadn't at all. At least I couldn't see Caliope from the top of it. What I did see was a big snake that might have been five feet long if it hadn't been coiled and ready to strike. I had sense enough to know that it was a rattler, ready to strike. I backed off mighty quick and tried another way.

By this time I was getting worried. What if I couldn't find my way back to town? What if I ran into Indians? Maybe an outlaw?

The horseman came along a low spot in the ground at a canter. He was a big man, although maybe that was because I was only ten years old. He grew nearer and larger, until finally he came up a little rise and pulled in just in front of me.

"Howdy," I said, being mannerly and not wanting him to know how scared I was.

"You lost, son?" he asked in a rumbly voice.

"I went out for a walk," I told him. "Just to see what I could find."

He grinned. "Find any Indians?"

"Nossir."

"I know that. If you had, you wouldn't be here now." He shifted in the saddle. "Come on up behind me, and we'll ride back to town."

That was my first experience with Jim Hagen. He told me later that my mother had missed me, that in desperation she had asked one of her boarders to look for me, and that the boarder, who had only a sketchy idea of the country north of Caliope, had enlisted the aid of the saloon-keeper.

It was a bonanza, the whole experience, because when Jim returned me, he had a talk with my mother. Curiously, she had a great respect for him: he attended church services on Sunday, he kept his saloon closed on the Lord's day, and he was known as a man who didn't cuss or chew tobacco. She was prepared to discount the local rumor that he had lived by the gun down in Texas and the Nations.

Jim talked to her about the need of a boy to have a father, about the necessity to be careful about going out on the prairie alone and unarmed, and when she protested that we didn't own a gun, he suggested that he himself teach me how to shoot and hunt, how to find my way without a compass, and generally how to take care of myself.

From that time on, I spent Sunday afternoons with Jim Hagen, attending his school, you might say, and I suppose I learned pretty well, because I never forgot the things he taught me.

Jim and I went back a long way together.

"Howdy, Ma'am," I said. "My name's Charlie
Pease."

She nodded and then... turned over... the time...

6

There were only five permanent boarders at Mrs.
Durning's, including me, and I met them at breakfast. The harness maker stayed there, a lean man in
his late fifties who was bald and all hunched over
from sitting on a harness bench. Then there was Cal
Rogers, the gunsmith. Cal was small and compact,
and he had a big handle-bar mustache that looked
like it would overpower his face. His hands were big
for a man his size, and they were ingrained with oil
and graphite.

Tom Scott was the marshal — had been for ten,
twelve years — and he was a bear of a man with shoul-
ders so broad, he had to turn sideways to get through
the narrow doors of the boarding house. He gave me
a cold look and asked me directly when I planned to
leave. I told him it depended upon, but I didn't say
what. I remembered Tom from five years before, and
the only thing that stuck in my mind was that when
Pete Moffatt had beaten me up, he'd let it happen. I
guessed that Bill had bought him now, the way he
seemed to have bought everything else in Caliope.

The rest of them had eaten and pulled out, and I
was drinking a last cup of coffee, when a girl came
through the door and sat down. There were some
flapjacks left, and Mrs. Durning came in and set
down a nice platter of bacon and eggs.

"Howdy, Ma'am," I said. "My name's Charlie Pearse."

She nodded and thought it over. "I'm June Shelton," she said, "but most folks call me Whiskey."

I could see why. She had honey-colored hair and her eyes were amber, like when you hold a glass of good rye whiskey up to the light and look through it. She wasn't what you would call pretty, but she had a face with a lot of character to it. From what I could tell, she had a nice trim figure without any fat on it, and she had good strong hands with long, sensitive fingers.

"You do a lot of looking, Mr. Pearse. Maybe that's why you don't have time to say too much."

"Beg pardon. I didn't mean to stare."

She smiled then, and there was no prettier sight I'd seen since I'd been in Caliope. "Looking's all right," she said. "So long as that's all it is."

"I never go faster than the track allows, Miss Whiskey."

She laughed and said she'd see me later. I didn't know where that would be, but I just nodded and told her I hoped she'd have a good day. I figured her for a milliner, but I wasn't about to get nosey. Not yet.

The swamper was still busy cleaning out the saloon when I went by, so I went ahead down the street, picking up the changes as I went. The old bank was gone, replaced by a neat stone building with a big plate-glass window in front. I remembered that Jim Hagen had said it was half Bill's and I guessed banking must have paid off pretty well for Bill and his partners to afford to build a stone edifice for their loot.

Sol Levitan was busy on my suit, and since I'd dropped by, he took some final measurements and had me try it on. I was happy enough with the way it looked, but Sol said he had to do more work on it. He was a perfectionist, was Sol.

By the time I got back to the saloon, the swamper was done and the first customers of the day were already having their eye-openers. I recognized Alf Benton, the banker, but the others were strangers to me. Jim nodded and motioned toward the back room.

I went on back and said good morning to Martha, who was drying the breakfast dishes. "Good to see you again, Charlie," she smiled. "Jim have a talk with you yet?"

"Not to mention. He told me to come on by this morning."

"Well, he's got something he wants to discuss with you, but it'll be a while until the bartender gets in and he's free."

"You hired a bartender? I didn't think there was that much business in Caliope."

"There is now," she said shortly. "You see, we're on the stage route between the Kansas Pacific and the Santa Fe, so a lot of stage travelers come by. They generally stay overnight at Mrs. Durning's, and some of them come in here. It's pretty near as good as being on the railroad, and there's some talk of a spur line coming down through here. If that happens, I'd guess we're going to be the county seat, and then let her buck!"

About that time Jim came in and helped himself and me to a cup of coffee. "Set," he said. "Take the load off your feet."

I sat down and sipped at my coffee.

"You want something stronger," Jim said, "just you name it."

"Don't drink that much, Jim, and never in the morning. I stick to coffee, mainly."

He nodded his approval. "What I had in mind, Charlie, was for you to come in and play a little poker with whoever's around. You could have a table in the back there, and it would give us both a nice little income."

"Sounds good so far. Poker's what I do best. What did you figure the take to be?" It was usual for the saloonkeeper to charge a set amount for the use of the table or to take a percentage.

"Well, some days you won't be doing much business, and then there's other days you'll be doing pretty well. I'd say a percentage would be fair, maybe ten percent of what you win. If you lose, you take the loss yourself."

I'd seen saloons where you had to pay out fifty dollars a day to rent a table, although twenty-five was more usual. Ten percent was a much better deal, because it took into account the bad days as well as the good.

"That sounds pretty good to me, Jim." We shook on it, and then I said, "This is going to be poker only? Or some blackjack too?"

He smiled. "I already have a blackjack dealer."

I hadn't noticed him the night before, and I said so.

"It ain't a him, it's a her, and she goes by the name of Whiskey."

My mouth must have been open long enough to draw flies, because Martha laughed at me from over

47

the dishes she was putting away. "I guess you might have met her over at Mrs. Durning's this morning, Charlie."

"Yes'm, I did. She is purely beautiful."

Jim chuckled. "She is also one hell of a dealer. With her I take the same's I will from you. Ten percent. Now there's one house rule she stands by, and so will you. I want an honest game. No clipped cards, nothing from the bottom of the deck or any of that stuff. You are always the dealer, so nobody can pull a fast one on you, but that means they've got to trust you. If they don't, they won't come here to play, and we both lose out."

"That's the only game I play, Jim."

He nodded, satisfied. "Anytime you want to start, then, is all right with me. If you don't feel like working and you want to take a day off, I generally charge the boys five bucks for the table and the cards, so you won't hurt my feelings none."

"Fair enough."

"Coffee's on the house, but you pay for your own whiskey. If you want, I can give you a whiskey bottle with cold tea in it. That way you won't be tempted to break another rule. I don't want drunks dealing cards for me. A man gets drunk, he gets quarrelsome, and that won't work. The last thing I want is brawling or gunplay in here."

"Fair enough," I told him. "But I do wear a gun. Sometimes it stops arguments before they get started."

"Ever have to use it?"

"I never drew on a man, no. I hope I never have to."

He nodded, apparently satisfied. "One last thing,

Charlie. You came back here, which isn't the safest place for you to be, considering Pete Moffatt and his temper. I don't figure you came back to see your dear half-brother. So why are you here?"

I told him briefly about Deadwood Sam and his helpers. "I figured it might be a good idea if I stayed out of circulation for a while, at least as far as the big towns are concerned. I don't see any way they could follow me up here, Jim, but if they do, I'll get the hell out before there's trouble. I don't have a yen to get myself killed, and I sure as hell don't have a yen to kill another man."

And that's the way it stood for a while.

Whiskey came in later in the afternoon and took her place behind a table in the corner behind a screen. I went over and played a little blackjack with her to find out how good she was and to talk to her. Already we had something in common: we were both working partners with Jim Hagen.

She was good. Her table rules were the usual: dealer drew on sixteen and stood on seventeen. But even so, she was good enough to relieve me of ten dollars inside of an hour. "You have your odds down pretty good," I told her.

She smiled prettily. "Thank you, Charlie. I learned from a good man."

I thought a moment. "Stud Walker?"

Her mouth opened in surprise. "How'd you know?"

"Stud taught me all I know about poker. We never got around to blackjack, but I heard he was one of the best."

"That he was."

"How did you meet up with Stud?"

49

Her story was pretty common for that time and that place. Her mother was a refined person who intended to bring up June to be a lady. Her father had the same idea in mind, but his frustration at being an English gentleman in a country where English gentlemen didn't count for much led him to the bottle. He sold land for a while, Whiskey told me, and then he sold shares in town stocks — some of the towns even got built, too — and finally he was reduced to writing beautifully composed letters to his English relatives. The letters alternately asked for a financial stake or for a passage "home" for himself and his family.

Nobody answered the letters, so Whiskey never knew at the time if they were lost in transit, were addressed to non-existent persons, or if the recipients simply didn't care. This, she said, told her something about ladies and gentlemen. If money was the only thing that counted with them, then they weren't a whole lot different from the rest of us.

"Not that money's everything," she said. "It's not even much of anything, so long as there's enough to live on and a little over to help buy dreams."

I agreed and she went on.

Her mother had died of a heart ailment or frustration, take your pick, and she and her father moved into a boarding house. They had the two poorest rooms in the place, and for a time her father worked at schemes that would recoup the family fortune. Unfortunately, he was no better at scheming than he had been at making a living. They lived on a day-to-day basis.

"I think how he might have quit being a gentleman and gone into business in some little store or gone to work for the railroad or something. But he couldn't survive in the common world, being a gentleman."

"Never having been one, I wouldn't know," I told her. "Why didn't he try gambling? I've heard English gentlemen like to gamble."

"He didn't have the courage," she said curtly, and then she went on.

Father had sent out yet another plea for help, and this time he received an answer. It was short and to the point, she said: there was no money to send to a wastrel, to a man who had forgotten his proud heritage to the extent that he had begged. From now on, he would be dead to the family. There would be no further communication. At least, she said, the letter proved that there was a family.

That night her father shot himself, being considerate enough to do it outdoors where he wouldn't mess up the decor of his rented room. Whiskey found the letter the next day.

"He wasn't very strong, Charlie," she told me. "He couldn't cope with the things he had to cope with, and he'd never been trained to do anything—only to be a gentleman. When you have to live by your wits, you have to realize that somebody with fewer wits is going to be paying your way. Father couldn't accept this. He was a kind-hearted man, in his own way, you see."

I didn't comment on that. Kind-heartedness, like charity, ought to begin at home, and there wasn't much indication that Whiskey's father had shown his wife or daughter much consideration.

I changed the subject. "Didn't you ever consider getting married?"

"No, thanks," she smiled. "I couldn't see myself

giving up any chance I might have of independence just to buy a little future security. I saw what marriage to a weak man had done to Mother, and I vowed I'd never be put in that position."

She had considered millinery, perhaps sewing for someone who already had customers. There were no openings. Finally, she began to help with the work at the boarding house, doing washing and cooking and cleaning in return for her room and board until she could figure out what to do next. It was, she said, her finishing school: she learned enough there to know how to run a cafe or a boarding house, if she ever got enough money to set herself up in business.

That was when she had met Stud Walker.

At that time, Stud was a man in his late fifties, bald-headed and pop-eyed, and he had a mind like a steel trap. He could figure odds on a hand before the other players had picked up their cards. He wandered in on her one day in the boarding house while she was taking a rest, playing a game of solitaire.

"He saw something in me, I guess," she told me. "He asked me what cards were out against me, where they were, and how I knew, and I told him. Then he showed me how to play blackjack and told me how to figure odds. He said it was a good game to learn, but he didn't tell me at the time that he had an idea I could make money at it."

It was typical of Stud. He was a good card player, and he'd made a living with the pasteboards for years, but he was never too busy or too tired to teach a willing pupil, if there was any promise showing at all.

"What you have to do is make up your mind," he told her. "You are going to be a scrub-lady in a boarding house until hell freezes over, or marry a no-good rascal who'll run off and leave you, or you're going to make something of yourself. Now, which is it to be?"

"I'm going to make something of myself."

"Well, then. Every day for a month we're going to play blackjack until you've got the game down pat, and then I'm going to take you to a place I know and stake you."

She had made fifteen dollars that night, playing in the back room of the Alhambra Saloon in Topeka, and the rest followed. Stud moved on to Dodge, Whiskey moved on to Ellsworth, and eventually to Caliope.

We talked over coffee in her little alcove until Jim came over and coughed, a little self-consciously. "Somebody to see you out front, Charlie."

I followed him out into the saloon, and there was the marshal himself, Tom Scott. He had aged in the past five years, which is a silly remark, because everybody ages. But he had aged more than most. His hair had gone almost white where he wasn't bald, and the beginning of a paunch did battle with his belt. He was neatly dressed in black broadcloth trousers and a white shirt, and the shirt was clean. He held his black hat in his hand, like a man going to church and uncertain of what to do with it.

"Marshal," I said, waiting for him to make the first move.

"I've got to thinking about this morning," he said, and his voice boomed out of that big chest. "I asked you how long you were staying, and I figured you was smart enough to take a hint and move along. But now I find you're ready to set up business gambling."

53

"That's right. I never said I was moving on."

"My advice is that you do it. Pack up and get."

"Tell me why I ought to take advice from a man who stood by and let me get beat up?"

"Because it could happen again," he said flatly. "I didn't like to see it happen, Charlie, but it could happen again and there would be nothing I could do about it."

I stared at him to see if he'd flinch. He didn't, so I said, "Nothing's going to happen here unless Pete starts it. And if he does, I'm going to back off as far as I can."

"How far is that?"

"Far enough to stop a fight unless he tries to kill me. And then I'm going to kill him. I'm through running, and I'm through taking punishment for things I didn't do."

He didn't even answer that. He just grunted and turned to the new batwing doors and walked through them, seeming to fill the space of two men with his big body. He would have been a good man to have had on my side.

7

It was two days before Bill got up enough nerve to talk to me, and of course he didn't come down to the saloon. He sent his clerk down to the Emporium to ask me to come to supper. I told the clerk I'd be there, and Jim Hagen grinned. "Looks to me like you're going to get another invite to leave town," he said. "Either that or you're getting to be respectable."

"Let's wait and see."

Jim was free and clear, I guessed. Bill didn't own any piece of him, and so long as he ran an orderly place, there wasn't much Bill could do to him. If half the town was in favor of not having a saloon, the other half was in favor of having one, and Bill couldn't openly move against Jim without some repercussions. Or so I figured.

I cleaned up my boots and put on a clean shirt in honor of the occasion, and I wore my new broadcloth suit. It seemed to me like the least I could do.

Mary Lou was all sweetness and light, but I noticed she had only to look at Bill, and he did exactly what she said. Somehow I'd never figured her to have that strong a thumb. If it wasn't for the feeling I had that Bill had wanted me run out of town five years ago, I would have felt sorry for him. But then, you can't feel too sorry for a man who enjoys being bossed around.

We had a nice roast and baked potatoes and boiled carrots and greens, and to finish off with Mary Lou had baked a pie with canned cherries. I complimented her on her cooking, and I didn't have to fake a thing. She was a good cook and a good housekeeper to boot. She was even tactful: she had work to do, she said, and she knew we must have a lot of things to talk about. Perhaps we'd like to smoke a cigar in the garden, she said, which was her way of letting me know that no cigar smoke would ever pollute her home.

Bill offered me a big Havana, a banker's cigar, but I passed in favor of one of my skinny ones. There's no sense in a man getting used to something he can't afford to have around all the time. When it's gone, he misses it too much.

"I see the world's been treating you well," he said without preamble, and I was reminded of old Tom Scott getting right to the heart of the matter.

"I can't complain. I've made a few enemies along the way, I guess, but that goes with living, doesn't it?"

"Sometimes. Anybody in particular?"

"Outside of Pete Moffatt? A gambler back in Denver, for one. I relieved him of some money—honestly. He's not an honest man, so he resented it."

"Is he looking for you?"

I shrugged. There were some things about me Bill didn't have to know. "Could be," I said. "If he is, he's a damn fool."

"We have a nice quiet town here," Bill said reflectively. I could hardly see his face in the dusk, except from the glow of his cigar. "We don't want to change it."

56

"I wouldn't worry about it, Bill. I never yet killed a man, and I hope I never have to. I play an honest game, and no man's got just cause to complain against me."

"You carry a gun."

"And I'm good with it."

"What would you do if that man or someone like him came here looking for you?"

I shrugged. "If I had time, I'd get the hell out of the way. Move on, I suppose. If push came to shove, I'd kill him before he killed me. That's self-defense, and everybody's got that right."

"What about Pete Moffatt?"

"I'll handle Pete when the time comes. Maybe I can even talk some sense into him."

"How?" Bill laughed scornfully. "He's never going to forgive you for Sara's death."

"Maybe he's got the wrong target, did you ever think of that? I wasn't responsible for Sara getting in the family way, and I sure as hell wasn't responsible for her killing herself. One of these days, Pete's going to find out who the father of that child really was, and then I'm off the hook and God pity him when he gets what's coming to him."

"I don't know whether to believe you or not," Bill said, and he cast the end of his cigar away into the gloom.

"Up to you," I said, and the conversation was over. I knew nothing more than I'd known before: Bill wanted me out of town to keep the Pearse name free of the taint of gambling. On the other hand, there was nothing he could do about it if I minded my own business.

I thanked Mary Lou again for the good supper,

57

shook hands with Bill, and started back toward the Emporium.

Like I said earlier, Bill's house was out on the edge of town and the Emporium was clear over on the other side. The sidewalk didn't come out this far, the merchants of Caliope being unwilling to pay for boards even to oblige Bill Pearse, so I walked out in the road enjoying the shine of the stars and the gentle breeze coming from off the prairie. They brought back good memories of a lot of years ago when I'd been a kid coming back from a day's hunting.

I was just about opposite the hardware store when I heard a noise between the buildings to my right. It could have been a cat or a dog going after a bone, but something told me it wasn't. I took one more step, and then I ran straight toward the noise. It's something you have to teach yourself, to run at the danger instead of away from it, and the reason you do that is because it's unexpected. It gives you a little edge, and it's good for maybe a half-second. But it beats nothing hands down, like the fellow says.

There was a little noise, a click-clack, and I threw myself sideways just in time to escape the blast of a shotgun. The buckshot went past me close enough to hear and I heard the thunk when they struck a building across the street. I had my gun out by then, and I waited for the second barrel, but all I heard was the sound of running feet in the weeds and darkness behind the buildings.

Something stung my leg, like a beesting, and I knew I'd been hit. Not bad, probably, but I was in no shape to go hunting a killer in the dark. I put my left hand down and sure enough, there was a hole in my brand-new suit pants and my leg was all slippery with blood. Nothing broken, I hoped, and took a few tentative steps. No, nothing broken.

I hobbled on down to the Emporium, trying to stay away from lighted windows and trying to stay out of the center of the batwing doors when I went in.

"Some fellows here would like a game, Charlie," Jim said.

I nodded. "In a minute, Jim. I'm going to need a little help first."

His jaw dropped as he looked down and saw my leg. "I thought I heard a shot before. Who was it?"

"Damned if I know. He cut loose with a shotgun out of the dark, and I couldn't get a shot at him."

"Go in the kitchen and set down, and I'll get one of the boys to go fetch Doc."

And then Whiskey was there. "I'll handle it, Jim," she said.

8

I didn't play any poker that night. Whiskey and Martha slit my pant leg with Jim's straight-edge razor, washed out the wound with rye whiskey, and cut out the ball, which was right under the skin and no big thing. Once I was bandaged, Whiskey walked me back to the boarding house and ordered me to bed.

"Seems awful lonesome in here," I said. "Maybe you'd like to stay a while and keep me company."

But she only grinned at me and said that I wouldn't be good for a damn thing anyhow.

That kind of took me off balance, because I'd never figured she'd be interested. It shouldn't have, because there'd been something almost galvanic between us the moment we met. It was almost as if each of us had always known that there would be somebody some day who would be right, and that there would be nobody else ever.

Once we'd admitted that, it was no longer a question of whether, but of when.

The next day I hobbled down to the marshal's office, just on general principles, not figuring he'd be willing or able to do anything about the backshooter, but going through the motions for form's sake.

"I warned you," he said. "This ain't your town."

"You did that. Now I'm going to tell you something. The more people keep telling me that, the more determined I am to stay. There's something pretty fishy going on around here, and I'm going to wait around and see what it is."

"There's things a man's better off not knowing," he rumbled. "Not that that would stop you."

"Nope," I grinned.

He rummaged in a drawer and fetched out the office bottle and passed it over for me to sample. It was rye, neither good nor bad. I swallowed and he put down a belt, corked the bottle and put it back in his desk.

"I just want you to know, I didn't have nothing to do with that. I don't think Pete Moffatt did either. You might try to figure out who else would want you dead or out of here."

"I couldn't start to guess," I told him, and then I went back down to the Emporium to see if I could scare up a game.

News travels fast in a small town, and a lot of men drifted in and out of the saloon that afternoon to see the man who'd been shot. A few of them stayed to play poker with Poker Pearse. Even Jim hadn't been slow about passing the word around.

Of course business was all the better for it. There are some men who don't mind paying out a little money to say they've had the privilege of playing with the best, and I'm the kind of man who doesn't mind, so long as it's me who's getting paid.

Pete Moffatt and two of his riders came by for a drink and Pete glared at me. Jim kept close to the billy club he kept under the bar, but he said nothing. Pete downed his drink in a gulp and came over to the table where I was playing out a hand of seven-up

61

solitaire to keep my hand in.

"Remember me, boy?"

"I'm no boy, Pete. Yes, I remember you."

"Well, I stopped by to tell you I wasn't the one who back-shot you last night. I'm glad it wasn't worse than it was."

"Glad you feel that way."

"Because I want you whole and in one piece when I come for you. And when I do, it's going to be face to face, and I'm going to kill you."

I spread my coat a mite to let him see the butt of my gun. "You better be good, Pete, because I can take you."

"I'm never going to forget what you done to Sara."

"For the record, Pete, I never touched Sara. Before or after we were married. And her killing herself was her own idea, not mine. That's the last time I'm going to say it, so see if you can remember."

"You're a damn liar."

I shrugged it off. "I've been called worse and it never did me any harm. You've got an almighty hate, and I make allowance for it. But stay the hell away from me and save your hide."

"I hope some day you know how it feels to have somebody you love die young. Only I don't figure to let you live that long."

"Sure, Pete," I said, acting bored. But I made sure I watched his hands. That's the first rule of gunfighting: a man's eyes can't hurt you, it's what he does with his hands that counts.

But he only grunted and turned around and walked out. Jim shrugged and raised his eyebrows. "He don't forget a thing, Charlie."

That night Whiskey came to my room, just to talk. I had changed the dressing on my leg and decided that it was going to heal up just fine. Whiskey and Martha had done a good job cleaning it out, and it didn't amount to much more than a deep cut.

"You're lucky it didn't go over another inch or so," she said. "It could have broken your leg."

"I'm just lucky as hell sometimes."

"Count your blessings, Charlie."

I changed the subject. "Ever feel like riding out of this town and seeing some country?"

"Love it. I try to ride on Sundays when Jim's closed up."

"Fine. How about next Sunday then? There's an old fellow up north of here I used to know. I'd like to drop out and see him. We could rent a rig and take a lunch along."

She laughed, a bubbly infectious laugh that made you want to join right in, even if you didn't know what she was laughing at. "Charlie, I ride. I don't get driven like a fancy lady."

"I don't suppose you'd want to come a little closer. I don't bite."

"No, I wouldn't. You get that leg of yours healed, and I'll come a lot closer on Sunday."

Not much happened the rest of the week. I hobbled down to the store to see Bill, partly because he hadn't come around to see me, although the whole town had heard about my getting shot, and partly to get some exercise to keep the leg from stiffening.

The clerk was there, and he stayed close to the till and the sawed-off. I was a dangerous character. "Bill's gone," he said. "He had some business down

63

in Wallace."

I bought a fresh supply of cigars and matches, and then I went over to Sol Levitan's.

Sol commiserated with me awhile, saying what a shame it was somebody had shot me, and did I know who it was.

"Hell, Sol, I have no idea. It looks like Caliope's declared open war on Charlie Pearse. I'd have to suspect half the town."

"Pete Moffatt?"

"He came by special to tell me it wasn't him. He said he wanted it face to face, when the time came, and somehow I believe him. He wants the satisfaction."

Sol shook his head. "A bad business. Charlie, did you ever think of moving out? Going someplace else?"

"I don't run any more, Sol. I ran out of this town once, and now everybody thinks I had something to do with Sara's dying. I'm not going to make that mistake again. There's something crazy going on here, and I'm going to find out what it is."

"Don't get yourself killed doing it," he said laconically, and then we talked about trivial things for a while. I wasn't going to get any information out of Sol. Maybe he didn't have any to give.

That night Jim came over to the table during a lull. "You figure out who took that shot at you yet?"

I shook my head. "Hell, the whole town's hoping," I told him. "It could have been any one of them."

"Who's stirring up the town?" he asked quietly.

"Moffatt, probably. He's the one has a hate for me."

64

Jim shook his head. "I think he was telling the truth when he said he didn't. I think the one you got to watch out for is the man who fathered Sara's child."

I put down the deck of cards I was riffling and stared at him. "Why would he? Hell, I took the blame and I got the shame. I don't think there's anybody in town except you and Sol knows any different. And you don't really know—you just believe me."

"You aren't thinking, Charlie. There's three people really know, only one of them's dead. You know you weren't, and one of these days you're going to start wondering who it was, and maybe you'll even find out. And that's the day the shit is going to fly."

"So he wants me out to keep his name clean?"

"That's the way I'd figure it. I'd also figure that he didn't try to hit you the other night, or he wouldn't have missed. That shot was kind of a warning, like. He might have run out of warnings though, and that's why you've got to watch out."

Just then the evening started to move. Two riders came in and made for the bar, and a drummer and four city types came in the side door from the stage station. Whiskey drew one of them, the drummer, for her blackjack game, and three of the others followed after they'd primed themselves. I bided my time. After all, I had all night.

It was a good night, once I got a game going. I didn't play for blood, but I came out eighty dollars ahead, eight of which went to Jim. Saturday night would be better, in a sense, because that was the night the locals would drop around for the big game of the week. But in another sense it would be worse: you couldn't take money from locals the way you could from stage passengers. If you did, eventually you'd find yourself out of a game, or else the locals would play privately in some other place, and Jim would lose the trade. Either way, I lost.

I thought about what Jim had said, and the more I thought the better sense it had made. I told Whiskey about it when we walked back to Mrs. Durning's that night, but she told me not to go looking for crazy reasons when I had Bill to blame. "He's the one who's got most to lose if you stay here," she said. "You were the black sheep and you went out and made it on your own anyhow."

"Bill wouldn't do anything like that," I said. "Hell, he's my half-brother."

"Cain and Abel were brothers too," she said.

"That was different. They were competing for the old man's flocks or something."

Whiskey merely grinned. " 'None so blind as they who will not see.' "

In a sense she was right, of course. Our father had left money to my mother, which was his right and his responsibility, and that must have caused some resentment on Bill's part. I've noticed too, that, no matter how much some folks get, they always want more. I tried to think of things Bill and I had done together when we were growing up, things I could bring to Whiskey's attention to prove that she was wrong. But the more I thought about it, the more I realized that we had never really done much together at all. Bill was trying to establish himself in business when I was still a kid. He was involved in ledgers and inventory and pricing, and I was interested only in hunting and fishing. It was almost by accident that I got involved in the store, partly because he must have felt he had to do something for an orphaned kid, and partly because my knack with figures was useful to him.

So we finally talked about the ride we were going to take the next day and avoided the subject of Bill by tacit consent.

9

The claim had been owned by Henry Picken, but when we got there it was deserted. Henry had improved it, according to law, by building a dugout into the side of a hill and fencing off twenty acres around the dugout. But now the fence was broken, rusted through in several places, and the dugout was empty. Henry had left a note of sorts pinned to the north wall: "Wish you better luck than I had. Henry R. Picken."

I was sorry, partly because I wanted Whiskey to meet Henry, who was as close a friend as I'd had when I got to be a young man. He'd taught me a lot about reading sign and hunting and shooting. He had been an Indian scout with Harney years before, and if he'd forgotten anything, I couldn't find out what it was.

The place was snug enough, provided you didn't mind a little ground damp or a stray snake or two. Henry had dug into the south side of a little hill and lined his cave with limestone slabs. Then he'd built out a little way from the cave to make a nice entrance with a door and two honest-to-God windows. It was warm in winter, cool in summer, and proof against bullets or arrows any time of the year. There was even a nice little fireplace in the north wall. The roof was the usual, cottonwood poles covered with slabs of turf, and an old, half-rotted tarpaulin kept most of the dirt from falling down into the room.

"I wonder why he left," Whiskey said.

"I suppose he couldn't make a go of it. Henry never had much money. Never enough to buy cattle, anyway. And you couldn't raise any crops on this kind of land. It's good for grazing, but that's about all. Hell, he couldn't even keep up much of a garden."

"Was he alone?"

"Yep. Never had a wife that I knew of. He made out hunting and getting a bounty on wolves and on his Army pension. But he wasn't getting anyplace except older."

She sat down on the edge of the bunk, two poles driven into the walls and supported by a third at the corner. "It's a good place to get started."

"Get started doing what?"

She grinned at me. "Start getting ahead in this world. A young couple might buy a few head of cattle and run them here. Maybe build a nice house some day and raise a family. I'll bet you could get some stock from one of the big outfits."

"I don't have any experience with cattle," I told her, and then I realized what we were talking about. "Are you serious?"

"Yes, Charlie," she smiled.

I wasn't sure I was ready to get married again, even to Whiskey. She was one hell of an attractive woman, and I figured one of these days we were going to go to bed together, but that's not the same thing as making a life-long commitment.

"Don't fret it," she said gently. "Just think about

it."

And that's all I did from then on out. The more I thought about it, the more I liked the idea. I had enough money to buy a few head and to buy the Picken claim, and in a year's time I'd have even more.

We talked about it that afternoon in the dugout, and then we rode out a way and looked over the land and talked about it some more, and by the time we headed for home or what passed for it, it seemed to me that it could happen very easily.

I was kind of glad we hadn't just hopped into bed by the time we got back to Mrs. Durning's. It was something to look forward to, you might say, and besides we had a lot more going for us than a sociable roll in the hay. I was getting to see Whiskey as a good, self-reliant sort of person, somebody special. She was no little girl waiting for somebody to take care of her; she was a strong-willed woman who was looking for a partner, not a boss, and she'd picked me. It made me feel kind of proud and humble, all at the same time.

The land up there at the old Picken claim was about as pretty as any you'd see. There was a little creek on the other side of the hill, and willows and cottonwoods grew there. Up a little farther, there were ash and hackberry trees, and the grass was long and lush. I didn't know much about cattle, but it struck me I could always sign on with Jim Thatcher for a few months and learn the rudiments. One thing I could see clearly was that a man wouldn't have to go broke here, if he just had enough money to stock a herd and used the common sense God gave him.

That's what I was thinking about that night when I went to sleep, and it gave me something to look forward to for the first time in years.

If Sunday was great, Monday was pure hell. Bill came down to the boarding house looking mighty solemn. He said he was glad I hadn't got hurt worse than I had, and he told me he was concerned about me. I told him I was touched by his solicitude.

"No need to get sarcastic," he snapped back. "It's not my fault you've got enemies in this town. Remember what you did."

I passed on the last comment. "No secret either that you'd just as soon I'd get out of town and stay out."

"Put yourself in my place," he growled. "I'm a respectable citizen and I've got plans."

"So have I," I grinned.

"The main reason I came down here is because I heard something in Wallace you probably ought to know. I had some business with Pete Robidoux, and he said two fellows were in his place asking about you."

"Did they have names?"

Bill looked at me for a long moment. "Would the name Sam Bonner mean anything to you?"

I wasn't going to give him the satisfaction of knowing I cared, so I shrugged and said, "Maybe, maybe not."

"Well, he was one of them. The clerk down there at the store told him you'd bought a big Fifty Sharps and that you were headed for Texas to hunt buffalo."

"Good a guess as any. Thanks for telling me."

"Don't mention it," he said in a huff, and then he walked out without so much as a so-long, see-you-later.

I wished I'd never told Bill that anybody was looking for me, but the damage was done now. The only thing I could hope for was that Sam and his gunslingers would head out for the Nations and get lost down there or involved in something so lucrative they'd forget about old Charlie Pearse and the money he'd won from them.

When Whiskey came down for breakfast, I was still working on my third cup of coffee, so I told her about Bill's visit.

"What are you going to do about it?" she wanted to know.

"Not a lot I can do, is there? Wait it out and see what happens."

"Wait for Sam Bonner and his partner to come up here and kill you? That's not too smart, Charlie."

I shrugged. "You're assuming he knows I'm here. Hell, he's most likely hunting me in Indian Territory right about now."

"Not if Bill has anything to say about it," she said as she ate her last piece of bacon. "Ten to one Bill left word where you could be found, and sooner or later you're going to have some company you don't need to have."

I didn't bother mentioning that Jim's boasting about Poker Pearse being available in the Emporium for a friendly game might have had something to do with Sam Bonner's arrival in Wallace. After all, a lot of people came through on the stage, stayed the night, and then went on to Wallace. I only said, "I can handle myself in a fair fight."

She twisted her head to one side and narrowed her eyelids. "Who ever promised you it would be fair?"

There she had me. It would be about as fair as the time old Pete Moffatt beat the tar out of me.

"And if you're counting on your pal Tom Scott, our revered marshal, to back you in a pinch, just remember that he let Pete Moffatt work on you. You've got me and you've got Jim Hagen, and that's the size of it."

"Sol Levitan too."

"All right, Sol. What's he going to do against a fast gun?"

I opened my hands palm out in surrender. "All right, honey. What do you have in mind?"

"First of all, get out of here. Don't tell anybody where you're going, don't let on that Bonner's after you. Just go."

I knew pretty much where I'd go. Up to the old claim, where I'd have a roof over my head and a good chance to defend myself if I was followed. For all Sam would know, the earth had opened up and swallowed Poker Pearse.

Whiskey knew too, because in the next breath she said, "I can ride up to see you and let you know what's happening. When it's safe, maybe you can come back. In any case, I can come join you later. If you want me to, that is."

"I want that more than anything else," I told her. "One way or another, we're going to make a go of it."

And so it was settled. I guessed I had a couple of days before Sam would figure out he was barking up the wrong tree and come up to Caliope. That was, if he hadn't talked to Bill personally and got his facts straight even before he left for Texas or the Nations. I told Jim I was going away for a while, and he told me I was welcome to come and run a game any time at all. "Don't want to mind your business, Charlie, but why are you pulling out?"

73

It sounded pretty close to silly, but I told him anyway.

He nodded. "Now you're acting smart. If this Bonner is after you, you'd best not be here when he arrives. You've got enough to worry about with Pete. Hell, Charlie, you can't take on the whole town."

"Don't aim to. I might wander down to Hays City and see what's doing around there. When these fellows give up on me, I'll be back. I still have some unfinished business to tend to around here."

Jim stroked his big mustache and led the way to the back, where Martha poured us a couple of cups of coffee and left us in peace.

"I hate to run away from trouble," I told him. "Seems to me I ran out of here five years ago. Then Deadwood got too rough for me. Then Sam Bonner ran me out of Denver City. Now he's doing it again. It seems to me like it might get to be a habit, and I wouldn't want to have that happen."

"When you get a little older, Charlie, you're going to realize that your life is more important than a lot of things. I'd like you to be around for your wedding."

Martha snickered from across the room where she was thumping away at a mound of bread dough.

"Hell, I've seen you and Whiskey making sheep's eyes at each other. It's no secret from me and Martha. And I say, God bless you both. You two have had some rough times, and you're good people in spite of it. You deserve to get a chance to make something of your lives."

There wasn't much I could say to that. I thought it was the kind of speech my Pa might have given me if he'd lived.

"I wouldn't even count on coming back here to clear up old trouble, Charlie. You probably won't get anywhere with it, and you could wind up dead, even without Sam Bonner's help. Take what you've got and be happy you've got it. You know and I know that you didn't do nothing wrong, and that ought to satisfy you."

"Sounds like good advice, Jim. I might take it after all."

10

That night when I got done at the poker table, I went up to my room and packed my suit and good shirts and put them on top of the sack containing my share of our nest egg. Whiskey watched me, handing me things from time to time. It wasn't what you'd call the happiest of occasions.

There wasn't an awful lot to pack, truth be told. I had the reloading equipment for the Sharps and the Starr, an old ambrotype of my folks that I generally kept on me, and the money, which I'd been converting into gold eagles and double eagles. That and a razor and comb about finished it.

"I'll ride out to see you next Sunday," Whiskey said. "By then we'll know more about it."

"I wish you could come with me now."

"I wish that too, but it's better if I stay here and see what's happening. It may be nothing at all, but we've got to know what we're up against."

I had to be content with that.

She went up to her room and I blew out the lamp and opened the window to get the stink of coal-oil out of the room before I went to sleep. The clean cool air came in from the prairie, hinting of winter, and I thought about how it would be when Whiskey and I got out of town and settled in on the Picken place. I'd have to go and file a notice to buy and put down my money, but it was almost as if the place was ours already.

I took a last look at the silvered hills north of town, and suddenly I froze. Something had moved down in the yard behind the boarding house. Cautiously I backed away from the window far enough to keep light from shining on my face, and then I scanned the yard, foot by foot, until I saw somebody standing next to the cottonwood tree at the edge of Mrs. Durning's garden.

My room was at the back of the house where it was quiet. I was almost certain that somebody else would be watching the front of the house as well. And I was positive that in fifteen minutes or less one of the two watchers would be coming into the house and walking up the stairs to my room.

I guessed that they would be positioned to cover the sides of the house as well; the man in the back was far enough over to cover the west side, and the man in front would be covering the front door and the east side as well. That ruled out any crawling out a side window. For a moment I thought about going down the hall to Tom Scott's room and asking for help, but it didn't take me long to figure out that it wouldn't be a good idea. Even if the marshal was in, he wasn't apt to risk his life to help me. For all I knew, in fact, he was in on the plan to get Pearse.

There was only one thing left to do and I did it. I took my saddlebags down the hall to Whiskey's room, tapped on the door and waited for her to open it.

"It's me, Charlie," I whispered when she came to the door, and in a moment she threw back the bolt and let me in.

She listened while I told her the situation, and then she said simply, "What do you want me to do?"

"Just stay put for a little bit. They're going to come in the house looking for me, I think. When they get inside, I'm going to try to get out a window and head for the livery stable."

"You'll never make it." She reached under her pillow and hauled out a Navy Colt. "If it's what you think, we can take care of it here and now."

"Hell, no! I'm not going to get you mixed up in this any more than you are already. Just stay put and don't let them in your room. If you can give a couple of convincing screams, that might do the trick, but let them get inside the house first."

She nodded and sat down on the edge of the bed, holding the Colt on her lap. I tiptoed to the window and peeked out toward the front of the house. Sure enough, the man out there was far enough to the side to cover that too, although he probably couldn't see me at the window, since I was behind the curtain. As I watched, he started to move toward the front door, and in a moment he had disappeared from view. I gave him a little time, maybe a minute, and then I heard the creak of the first of the steps that led to the front door, and I knew it was time to go.

I dropped the saddlebags and the Sharps out the window into Mrs. Durning's chrysanthemums, and then I vaulted over the low sill and went after them. It was only an eight-foot drop, but my knees came up to meet my chin, and I saw some stars that aren't ordinarily in the sky. I had about enough sense left not to move, in case one of the men had heard me drop, and sure enough around came the fellow from the rear of the house to see what was going on. I

78

watched him through a screen of spyrea branches until he decided nothing was wrong and went back to make sure nobody tried to sneak out the back door.

Right next to me I could hear somebody going up the stairs, and it seemed like about the best time there would be for me to make tracks.

I put a couple of houses between me and Mrs. Durning's, and then I legged it for the livery stable. I went in slow and easy, because I knew Sam had had two helpers back in Denver, and if he hadn't been too mad at the one fellow I'd taken with me for a train ride, he might have a third man waiting at the stable. But luck was with me just about the time I needed it. Joe Huntly, the hostler, was snoring away like a brass band in back, and nothing moved except the horses. They moved easily and unhurriedly, and that told me nobody was lurking there.

I took my time saddling, to get everything right, and secured the saddlebags, and then I looked around for strange horses. I spotted two right off; they were still hot from traveling, so hot I could smell them. Next to them on pegs were the saddles. I guessed Sam and his friend would be traveling light, and they might even have taken their saddlebags with them.

Somebody yelled out from the direction of Mrs. Durning's, and I pulled out my pocketknife and went to work. First, I cut the stitching almost loose on each stirrup, and then I loosened the stitching on the girths so they'd tear loose if anybody yanked too hard.

That was about all I could do in the time I had, so I led my bay out the back door, leaving the altered saddles for Joe to explain.

About a mile north of Caliope there is a ridge from which you can see three sides of the town. I unsaddled the bay and tethered it on the north side of the ridge, where there was good graze, and then I stretched out on the ground where I could see whatever there was to see. From time to time I napped, although it was pretty cold at one point. There was no point in running off to the dugout until I had figured out what Sam had in mind. I guessed he'd search the town systematically until he was satisfied I had gone, and then he'd probably come out looking for me in other towns nearby. When he didn't find me there, he'd probably return to Caliope to see if he could catch me napping.

For a while I told myself I'd outsmarted him, that if I only watched my back trail I could always stay ahead of him. But then I started thinking another way. He'd managed to chase me out of town, something even Bill and Pete Moffatt hadn't been able to do so far. That put me back to where I'd been five years ago when I'd run away from trouble, only then there'd been the excuse that I was an eighteen-year-old kid running from a combination of things I couldn't handle. Now I didn't have that excuse. I'd told myself, just like I'd told Bill and Tom Scott, that I didn't want to bring trouble in with me. But I guessed the real reason was one I didn't want to face. I wasn't ready to die, and a showdown with Sam Bonner could only end one way. He was ready to kill me to get hold of my money, and I wasn't ready to kill him. It was as simple as that.

I hung around the back side of the ridge until the moon went down and dawn came sneaking around the eastern sky, and nobody came or went who looked remotely like Sam Bonner. I waited some more, while the day blossomed out and the sun warmed the chill from my bones, and there was still no sign of anybody leaving town. If he'd pulled out, he'd have had to go out on the south side, following the trail that would eventually take him back to Wallace. Otherwise I would have seen him.

Naturally, I had all kinds of time to think of how Sam had traced me to Caliope, and the best answer I could come up with was one I didn't like at all. Bill had gone to Wallace for the express purpose of letting it be known that Poker Pearse could be found dealing nightly at the Emporium in Caliope. He had made sure to tell it in Robidoux's store, which was a natural clearing house for gossip and news. What was even worse, I'd given him the weapon by telling him I was being chased by someone who'd lost money to me.

There's not much you can do about a thing like that except learn from it. Mulling it over, time after time, is only a form of self-pity, and I wasn't having any of that. A person would be better off turning up his toes and dying. It's at least quicker.

There was a nice tang of October in the air, and when the sun went down it got downright chilly. I saddled the bay and rode east, keeping out of sight of town, until I cut into the stage road leading down from the Nebraska line. I followed that until I came to the little creek that cut a line south of town, and then I followed the creek until I came into the bushes just behind Bill's store.

I tied the bay to a sapling, crawled up the bank, and made my way between buildings until I got a clear view of the main drag. Just across from me lights were still burning in Sol Levitan's store, and voices came from the Emporium, a couple of hundred feet to the east. The marshal rode down the street, east to west, making his usual rounds. He would check doors on the stores that were closed, and then he'd ride down the alleys to make sure nobody was getting robbed, raped, or murdered, and then he'd ride back to his office for a cup of bitter coffee. His next round would be at midnight.

Sam would probably be in the Emporium picking up some spare cash before he headed out, unless of course he'd already left town by the south road. One way or another, I wanted to find out just what I was up against.

Tom Scott turned his horse toward the alley north of Main Street, and I walked across the street, following him at a distance, and feeling about as naked as a jaybird. But nothing happened. I followed Tom a couple of hundred feet back until I got to the back door of the Emporium, and then I knocked softly and waited for somebody to let me in.

11

Martha Hagen opened the door. As soon as she recognized me, she put a finger to her lips and motioned me in. Out in the saloon somebody was trying to sing "The Rose of Tralee" and making a real mess out of it. There were the usual loud voices and occasionally the clink of coins on the bar, and slap of cards and chips on the tables.

"They're here," she said. "Jim said they told him they were going to hang around awhile."

I nodded. "It figures. Is Whiskey all right?"

"She's fine," Martha smiled. "I don't think she ought to come back here just now though. You'd better stay clear of her until these men leave."

"I know. I was just asking."

She slashed at a loaf of bread, a slab of pickled beef. "You probably haven't eaten all day, have you? Here, take this with you."

I thanked her and made my way out. I didn't want to put anybody in danger any more than I had already.

I ate the sandwich sitting on the steps at the back of Levitan's store, and then I walked back down the alley the way I'd come, keeping out of the moonlight and hugging the buildings. I made it past the barber shop, and I was beginning to get the idea that things were going to work out just fine, when the door in the back of the jailhouse opened and Tom Scott stepped out.

I froze in a patch of shadow, but it didn't do me any good. The marshal chuckled and said, "Come on out, Charlie. It's time we had a little talk."

I followed him into the office, past the one cell made of two-by-fours laid flat and spiked together, and the other one of frame and chicken-wire for drunks who needed a place to sleep it off. The marshal motioned me into a chair and handed me a cup of coffee.

"I suppose you come around to see what was cooking," he said flatly. "Did you find out?"

"They're still here, if that's what you mean."

"That's exactly what I mean. You came here and they followed you. And now I'm stuck with a tinhorn gambler who's fast with a gun and two thugs he drug in with him."

I shrugged. "That's not my fault. I sure as hell didn't invite them in."

"I don't care whose fault it is, Charlie, but I want you out of here. I want you long gone and far away, because that's the only way I'm going to get rid of them."

The coffee was as bitter as I'd remembered, but it was hot and it helped wash down the sandwich Martha Hagen had made me. "I suppose you have something to tell them when I leave?" I said.

He nodded, real pleased with himself. "I'm going to tell them I seen you leave early tomorrow morning, and then I'm going to tell them a man on the stage seen you sloping along headed on the Wallace trail."

"That's nice and thoughtful of you."

"My advice is, don't head for Wallace, because

that's where they're apt to start looking."

I finished the coffee and stood up. "I don't much like running."

"Seems to me you've done enough of it so you ought to be getting used to it," he said unkindly. "On the other hand, I don't know that I'd fault you for running from this one. He's mean and he's fast, and he's got a couple of friends who come pretty close to him."

"You don't need to tell me," I said, and I walked out the back door again and snuck in between buildings until I was safely past the danger zone where Sam Bonner and his shootists might be looking for me.

There was a light on in Bill's house, and the glow of a cigar in the dark showed me that Mary Lou had banished him to the garden to have his smoke. I slipped down to the creek without his noticing me though, and then I worked my way back to where I'd left the bay and all my worldly possessions.

I don't know what I would have done if it hadn't been there, but luck was riding with me that night, and nothing had been touched. I'm not completely simple: I'd buried the sack with the money under a pile of dead leaves. It's one thing to lose your horse and your saddle and rifle, but to lose your money too would be a little more than a fellow would want to handle.

What Tom Scott didn't know, although he might have guessed, was that I had no real choice in where to go. If I wanted to see Whiskey again, I was going to have to make tracks for the old Picken claim and hole up there until she could get away to see me and we could make other plans. That could take a long time, especially if Sam Bonner got an idea that Whiskey and I were working together.

I rode through the night with the moon shining just as bright as you please, and I didn't meet a soul all the way to the wide valley that I used to come into the claim. It was kind of a good omen, I thought, but just to be on the safe side I stopped short of the dugout and settled down for some sleep before I went the rest of the way.

When I awoke, the sun was just coming up and the meadow-larks were singing. I was cold and hungry, and the ground was no match for Mrs. Durning's bed, so I was stiff as well. The first thing to do was to get me some staples so I could lay in for a while without having to go out and buy anything. I thought about my choices, and there weren't but two. I could head northeast to a little hamlet called Prescott, or I could head northwest to another little town called Montezuma. I picked Prescott, mainly because I'd heard somewhere that the hide hunters used to buy their supplies there.

I took enough money out of the sack to buy whatever I might fancy, and then I buried the sack by kicking down the side of a bank where a gully had washed out. It was a good place and easy to find again, because there was a big rock just beside it and a willow tree just behind.

I bought what I needed in Prescott, flour and salt and coffee and bacon and cheese, and then I asked the storekeeper about stray Indians north of there. He grunted and allowed as how he didn't know anything about any Indians, stray or otherwise. I wanted him to ask me where I was headed, but he didn't, so I left it alone. If I'd told him I was headed for Dakota

Territory, he'd have remembered that when Sam Bonner got around to asking him. This way when Bonner got around to checking, he'd guess I was headed north and it would be more believable.

Or so I hoped. I rode out of Prescott headed north and continued for three miles, until I was out of sight of the village, and then I circled around and rode back to the dugout, coming in some four hours later.

For the next week I played hermit. I paced out distances and set up marks to learn to handle the big Sharps, and finally I got it down to where I could hit a limestone slab two feet wide at two hundred yards. I suspected the Sharps was much better than that: I just wasn't up to controlling that big a rifle. On the other hand, I knew I could hit a man at two hundred, and that was good enough.

There was game to be had, and I ate pretty well. I got a duck with the revolver one night, and then I took an antelope with the Sharps. The cooking wasn't what you'd call home, but it wasn't half-bad, mainly because by that time I was hungry enough to eat it.

Whiskey came riding out the following Sunday. I spotted her two miles from the dugout, because I'd been riding a circle around the claim daily, partly to exercise the bay and partly to make sure nobody was sneaking up on me. I stayed where I was, just below the crest of a ridge, long enough to make sure nobody was following her, and then I rode down the slope to intercept her.

She looked tired and drawn, but she came into my arms with a happy cry. "I've missed you," she murmured. "Oh, Charlie!"

I was all too conscious of the stink of the dugout, the stale odor of fried meat and the reek of kerosene from the lamp, but Whiskey said it looked homelike and nice. It was a gray, lowering day, so I took a chance and made a small fire in the fireplace. The smoke would hang low to the ground and anyone seeing it at a distance might think it was ground fog, or so I hoped.

"They're still there," she told me. "All three of them."

"What do they do for money?"

"Sam's been cheating the regulars so they won't play with him any more, but he makes money off the stage passengers. The other two sit in on the games from time to time, but mostly they're gone. I think they're looking for you."

It made sense, after a fashion. Certainly Sam would want to know if I'd simply moved over to a nearby town or left the country. But outside of Prescott and Montezuma, there were no nearby towns. It surely wouldn't take them a week to find out all there was to find.

"More likely, they're waiting for me to come riding back," I told her. "I would guess they don't know about you and me."

"Don't count on it," she said sleepily, all snuggled up against me. "Whatever else Sam is, he's no fool. He keeps his ears open, and small towns gossip."

"Well, we'll have to figure on leaving."

"Leaving for where, Charlie? They'll only come after you again." She touched my face with her fingers. "I'm not blaming you for getting out—if you'd stayed there, they would have killed you. But you

88

can't run for the rest of your life."

If that was criticism, it was no worse than what I'd been telling myself. Already I was starting to grow up a little more. I was at least getting smart enough to know that you take your troubles right along with you when you run.

"Something else you ought to know about. They've got the town buffaloed. Even the marshal is scared of them. One of them went into Sol Levitan's store and ordered a pair of boots and went out without paying. When Sol said something about it, the man beat him up."

"And Tom Scott did nothing?"

"Nothing at all. They even went to your brother's store and took things and didn't pay. He was smart enough to put the stuff on a charge account so they wouldn't beat him up. But he's scared too."

"Serves him right," I said. "He's probably the one who got them to come to Caliope in the first place."

"That's my guess too. When he was down at Wallace, he probably left word that you could be found in Caliope, and that's all they needed."

"Do you know anything about them? I might as well know what we're up against."

"Not much. Just what I overheard. The short one with the red hair is Red James. I get the idea he was run off from Wichita some time ago and drifted north. He probably tied up with Sam in Deadwood or Lead, and he's been with him for some time. He's the one who ordered the boots and beat up on Sol."

I nodded. He was the one who'd been sitting in on the game in Denver.

"Then there's Dutch Evarts. He's stocky and stupid, but he'd be a dangerous man in a fight. He's

89

strong as a bull. I've heard of him before, I think it was in Abilene or Ellsworth. He was a friend of Ben Thompson's then."

"I didn't know Ben Thompson had a friend," I said, but I was worried. I'd seen both of them when I'd played poker with Sam in Denver, but I hadn't known who they were. Now that I knew, I wondered how I'd ever gotten away with kicking Dutch Evarts off a train. He'd gotten a reputation by shooting people for the sheer hell of it. I was up against three of the worst.

"What are we going to do, Charlie?"

"Wait another week. There isn't enough money around Caliope to keep them happy for very long. They're going to have to come looking for me or go to some town where there's more money. I'd guess they'll quit looking, at least around here, and move out. If we're lucky, they'll give up and take off for good."

I rode most of the way back to town with Whiskey, coming in from the west in case anybody was watching. But when we saw the street with its lights shining yellowly in the gloom, it didn't seem to me that anybody was out there looking for us. I kissed her goodbye, and she promised to come out to the claim the next Sunday, if she wasn't being watched.

And then I rode back across the prairie. The ride seemed twice as long as it had coming out, and long before I came to the valley where the dugout was, sleet was stinging my face and hands and rattling off my clothes.

There are times when you're alone, and then there

90

are other times when you're lonely. You can be lonely in a crowd, as far as that goes, and I've been down that long road before. But the time I spent alone in the dugout on the old Picken claim was not a lonely one. For one thing, I was busy figuring out how Whiskey and I could fix up the dugout to make it liveable until we could get a house built. For another, I was trying to find a way out of our Mexican stand-off.

The way matters stood, Sam and his pals were going to sit it out in the comfort of Caliope until they were satisfied I'd left the country for good. They weren't getting any closer to catching up with me, but I wasn't getting any closer to losing them, either. Somebody was going to have to make a move to break the stalemate, and I had a funny feeling that the first one to make the move was going to be the loser. There's a time to bet and a time to stand pat, and it seemed to me that this was stand-pat time.

When it came to thinking about fixing up the dugout, I did better. I had it figured out to the point where the house was built out as an extension of the dugout, connected to it for convenience. That way, we could use the dugout as a root cellar and as a shelter from the violent storms that occasionally roared through the High Plains.

All this figuring brought me back to thinking about Whiskey. Like any other normal man, I'd known a few girls in my time, but they had not been the marrying kind. I might be held in high esteem by fellow gamblers, saloon keepers, and dancehall girls, but that did me no good when it came to earning the respect of the less raffish members of society.

There were plenty of good men and women in the

society I moved in, but there were plenty of bad ones too, and I wasn't about to take on the job of making a "good" woman out of any of the dancehall girls I'd known, even if they'd wanted to let me tackle the job. To the best of my knowledge, none of them had, so we were kind of even on that score.

On the other hand, I had no hankering for getting hitched to somebody like Mary Lou. Jim had hit the nail on the head when he said she ran old Bill around like he was a little kid. It dawned on me during the time I spent alone in the dugout that what society called a respectable woman might wind up trying to do just that to me, and I wasn't about to let it happen.

For a long time I'd kept telling myself that one of these days a girl would come along who was just right. Somebody who knew my world and accepted it for what it was. Somebody who was basically decent and who respected herself and other people as well. It all added up when I met Whiskey. The "respectability" could come later, and with any kind of luck it would.

I've noticed over the years that there's nothing like a sizeable bank account to make folks respectable in the eyes of a town. You take a town of any size, and you'll find a fellow who uses coarse language, who dresses as he damn well pleases, who isn't afraid to call anybody from the mayor on down by his first name. Now if this fellow hasn't the price of a shot of whiskey, he's the town bum. He's somebody you cross the street to avoid. But if he's a tough-minded codger who set his brand on enough strays to build a herd and sell beef in steady supply, or if he's a conniver who found out where the railroad was going and bought up the right-of-way for ten miles, starving his wife and kids to scrape up the money, why then it's a different story. He's a go-getter, a first-rate citizen, and the worst thing anybody'll say about him is that he's eccentric, which covers a multitude of sins, like the preachers are fond of telling us.

I had it figured out pretty well in the time I spent in the dugout, there on the old Picken claim. With a little luck, Whiskey and I could be pretty well-off in five or ten years. We'd have enough money to be respectable in the eyes of Caliope, and very few people would have anything bad to say about the woman who used to deal blackjack in the Emporium or about the man who used to be called Poker Pearse.

If that's what we wanted. I wasn't sure I wanted to be "respectable" in the eyes of Caliope or anywhere else, as a matter of fact. I'd seen enough hypocrisy to know that Caliope wasn't any better or worse than any other town, and I didn't have to prove to anybody who I was, any more than Whiskey did. She was a good, decent, loving person, and that was good enough for me.

When it came to being respectable, Bill was a good example. He had made money, one way or another, and he seemed to own half the town. It was quite an achievement, for an honest man, to have done so in the space of maybe seven years. But nobody was going to stand up and say Bill Pearse had cheated him or that Bill Pearse was a no-good, low-down bloodsucker. No sir. Bill Pearse was a fine, upstanding citizen. A go-getter. And he wasn't even eccentric, which put the butter on the bread, you might say.

But when push came to shove, I'd take Sol Levitan

or Jim Hagen as a friend any day. Sol was half-way respectable, because he made a good living, but he was also a Jew, and that kept him outside the social pale. Not that he gave a damn, in all probability. He and his wife had a kind of society of two, and they respected each other and their places in it.

Jim Hagen filled a necessary role in Caliope, but a saloon-keeper he was, and a saloon-keeper he'd remain. He and his wife would never be invited to the home of Bill Pearse or the home of the president of the bank or the home of the local preacher. Even if there hadn't been rumors of Jim's former life in Texas — and nobody knew for sure — he'd be an ex-gunfighter and a saloon-keeper for the rest of his life.

I guessed that it would be pretty much the same with me and Whiskey. We might get enough money to get invited to a couple of homes, but basically we'd have to form our own society, and that suited me to a tee. There was nothing wrong with having Sol Levitan and Jim Hagen for friends, and there was a hell of a lot wrong with having people like Bill Pearse and Reverend Barnes as cronies.

12

Several times during the next three days I deliberately rode close to Caliope to see if I could see anyone out looking. I watched the stage road on both sides of town, and I even rode out on the Hays City road a couple of times, but the only people I saw were farmers coming to town for supplies.

That didn't mean that everything was all right. It only meant that I wasn't in a place to observe what was really going on. I tried to look ahead to Sunday, when Whiskey would be riding out to spend the day with me, but it didn't help to dispel the feeling that I'd done the wrong thing by running. I could hear my mother telling me that running never solved anything, that a person had to stand up and face his troubles, whatever they might be.

I spent Monday night and Tuesday night mulling it over, but at the end of them I couldn't see where I could have done anything other than what I'd done. If I'd stayed in Caliope and faced three expert shootists, I'd be planted in the little sun-baked cemetery by now. I had had no support ever from the marshal, who seemed to be as scared of Sam Bonner and his two henchmen as I was, and that wasn't even considering Pete Moffatt and his abiding hate for me. When it came down to the wire, all I could count on for friends were Sol Levitan and Jim Hagen.

Monday was a clear day, and the sun soon melted off the sleet that had drifted into pockets in the rocks. But Monday night a keen wind came out of the northwest, a sure sign of bad weather to come. Tuesday was gray and lowering, and Tuesday night I could hear the rattle of ice crystals against the chimney, and when I looked outside it was snowing lightly.

I had picked up a couple of rabbits during the day, and as soon as it was dark enough so nobody could see smoke coming from the chimney, I built a fire, put on a pot of creek water, and cut up the rabbits for stew, along with some wild onions and flour dumplings. That can be mighty good eating, especially if there isn't anything else to eat.

Just about the time I figured either the stew was ready or I couldn't hold out any longer, I heard a noise outside. I buckled on my belt and drew the Starr and went to the door and listened. Sure enough, somebody was tying up to the old hitching rack outside. I unbarred the door and stepped to one side. I wasn't dumb enough to open the door and present them with a perfect target.

I leveled the revolver and waited a couple of eternities, and then the door swung open and Whiskey called, "Hello!" and walked in.

I lowered the gun, feeling like something of a damn fool, and she grinned. "Expecting somebody else?"

"Not you—that's for sure." I helped her out of her heavy coat and took her in my arms. "This is where you belong," I told her.

"I know that," she said softly, and then she pushed me away. "I have some news. Sam and his friends packed up and rode out this morning."

"Which way did they go?"

"Sam told Jim they were going to look for you over east, maybe in Ellis or Hays City. They rode out east toward the stage road, so I think they might have been telling the truth."

I thought about it. There was no reason they couldn't have gone exactly where they said they'd go, but there was no reason either why they couldn't have ridden off a couple of miles to the east and then cut back to the same ridge I'd used, to watch the town.

"Did you check your back trail when you headed out?" I asked her.

She shrugged. "I looked behind me a few times when I left. I didn't see anybody."

"Did you cut a loop? Swing off to the side and watch your trail to see if anybody was following it?"

She shook her head. "I didn't think of doing that."

The gambler in me was shaking his head. The odds were on that she hadn't been followed, especially in a storm that would cover tracks fifteen minutes after they'd been made, but the penalty for being wrong was too great to make the bet.

"All right, honey," I said. "Let's eat this stew and get the hell out of here."

"You think I was followed?"

"I don't know, but I don't want to hang around here and find out. We can double back to Caliope and take a chance, or we can ride farther north and try for Nebraska. It'll be a hard ride with this weather, but we could probably get up to Platte Bridge easy enough. Or we could strike west to Julesberg."

"Caliope," she said immediately. "We can stay off to the side of the trail I made."

It made some kind of sense. If she'd been followed, Sam wouldn't expect me to return to Caliope. I might even get lucky and spot him on the way, and that would tell me a lot. It would tell me if I could stay in Caliope for a while, or whether we'd have to move right out.

"Caliope it is," I said, and then we shared out the stew and ate from the pot and the single plate, taking turns with the fork and spoon in a neighborly fashion, just like an old married couple

When we finished, I packed what I thought we'd need and stowed the rest of the gear in a corner. I was taking only my clothes, the Sharps, and the reloading tools; the rest could stay for the next fugitive who needed a place to hide. I had the money too, of course; I'd dug it out before the snow could cover the hiding place on the sound notion that you can't go too far wrong traveling with money.

"What about the fire?" Whiskey asked.

"Leave it. If you were followed, it won't tell them anything they don't know already."

Privately, I didn't think she had been followed. The night was pretty stormy, and from what I'd seen Deadwood Sam and his shootists were more at home in a barroom than they were out on the open prairie. There was a long moment in which I debated the wisdom of heading out into the storm myself. We would have a long, cold ride with danger waiting for us every step of the way. But there are times when it's better to move than to stay; I thought this was one of them.

I picked up the saddles and she opened the door for me, and there they were, just visible against the snow. I dropped the saddles and made a lunge for the door, but the guns roared and flashed and I felt a searing pain in my head, and then I fell forward into darkness.

It must have been after midnight when I came to. The snow had stopped and the stars were burning brightly in the sky. The saddles were gone, and when I looked, so were the horses. A great dark spot in the snow showed where I'd bled, but when I got enough nerve to touch my head I could feel only a crease along the side. The ball had missed killing me by a cat's whisker, which is enough to make the difference.

I made a maximum effort and scrambled to all-fours, and then I crawled to the doorpost and hauled myself upright. Inside the dugout the fire was still burning and the lamp was still lit. Whiskey lay crumpled in a corner, and I went over to her. She had been hit in the chest, just under the left breast, and when I bent over her I could see a tiny bubble form on her lips. A lung wound, probably. I went down on all-fours again and straightened her out, and then I pulled her dress apart to examine the wound. It was a clean hole, and when I felt around in back, there was an exit wound as well, nowhere near as neat and clean as the entrance one.

Soft lead slugs tend to do that.

The two dress shirts I wore to play cards were clean, and I ripped one up, sponged off the wounds with water from the canteen near the saddlebags, and bound pads around the wounds with a strip torn off the other shirt.

"Is it bad?" she asked.

"It could be better," I admitted.

"Lung?"

"I'm not sure," I hedged. "I've got it strapped up."

"How about you?"

"I'm all right. Creased my head and knocked me out for a while, is all."

She was silent for a long while, and then she said, "I shouldn't have come. They were waiting for me to do that."

"It's all right. They would have found me sooner or later. The real mistake was in running. I could have taken them on separately, and I probably would have made it."

She said nothing after that, and I realized she'd passed out again. After a while I got enough strength back to put her on the bed and cover her with my coat and the blanket.

Sam and his boys had done a thorough job of ransacking the place. The lamp and the food I'd left in a corner were all right, but the saddlebags had been dumped in the middle of the floor. The money, which I'd removed from the hiding place near the rock along the creek, was gone of course, but everything else seemed to be there. They had left the Sharps, probably because it had been too heavy to haul around, and my Starr was still in the holster.

I puzzled it out finally. The Starr was an ugly-looking weapon, nowhere near as graceful as a Colt or a Remington, so nobody wanted it. There had been no thought of disarming us, because in the dim light from the fire we had appeared to be dead. And damned near were, I thought. They'd found the money, which was what they were really after, and they'd taken the horses, which they would abandon somewhere on the prairie. After a while the horses would return to the livery stable in Caliope or someone would appropriate them, and the worst anybody would think would be that we had been killed in an accident somewhere out on this prairie. In a week everybody would have forgotten about the black sheep of the Pearse family and about Whiskey, the girl who used to deal blackjack at the Emporium.

My head had stopped bleeding, but I kept walking in and out of reality, like somebody in a room with one candle that keeps flickering and guttering, and that shows everything in a wavery and feeble light. I got to the fire and hauled the pot away, burning my hands as I did so, and then I took it outside and packed it with snow, so we'd have water to drink when the canteen went dry. While I was at it, I washed off the wound alongside my head with snow, and then I bound another strip from the shirt around it to keep it clean.

In another day or so, I'd be all right. I knew how concussions worked. Whiskey was another matter. If the slug hadn't done too much internal damage, she'd be better in the morning, and there would be hope. If it had, she'd be dead.

When the chips are down and you've made your draw, there's only one thing to do: play the hand you've got. There's no time for sentiment, only for reality. And reality had just struck in spades. Part of me thought about the good life Whiskey and I could have had together, but the other part of me thought about what would happen if she died. I'd go on living, of course. It's only in story-books that somebody pines away and dies because a loved one is gone.

I put some of the water in the coffeepot and brewed up some of the left-over meat and crumbled crackers in it. It would be nourishing enough for Whiskey when she came to. I left it simmering, built up the fire, and stretched out on the floor and went to sleep.

There was nothing else to do.

13

The next day it snowed again, not quite a blizzard, but close enough so you couldn't tell the difference unless you were an expert on Kansas weather. Whiskey was still unconscious, and for a long, horrible moment I thought she might be dead, but then I saw the faint rise and fall of her chest. She was hanging on, just barely. I remembered a story I'd heard about the Rebel guerilla leader, John Singleton Mosby, and how he'd been shot through both lungs and left for dead, only to recover and lead his men on still other raids against Union troops. Maybe Whiskey would be lucky that way too.

In a way, we'd already been lucky. We were both alive and our enemies thought we were dead. We still had weapons and a little food, and when the snow let up I'd be able to do a little hunting. Maybe I'd get lucky and find another antelope or a deer. Rabbit stew makes good eating, but Whiskey would be going to need good red meat to make up for the blood she'd lost.

"Charlie?" she murmured, and I went over to her. "It hurts when I breathe."

"Cracked a rib," I told her, although I wasn't sure. The ribs had looked all right to me. "You'll make it. Now I've got some nice soup for you to drink."

She managed to sip a little of the broth, and then she went back to sleep.

The snow let up toward noon, so I went down to the creek and followed it for maybe a mile before I got lucky and found what I was looking for. Three deer in a little clump of brush, busy feeding on branches. None of them was any great size, but the buck looked like an easy shot and I took it. He was facing me head-on, looking a little puzzled to see something on two legs out in the middle of all that snow, and I got a clean chest shot with the Sharps and dropped him in his tracks.

I dressed him out in the creek bottom and got him skinned before he froze, and then I put the heart and the best cuts in the skin and lashed it all together and humped it home.

Whiskey was awake and I told her about my success. She smiled and said she was feeling better, so I gave her the rest of the rabbit soup and commenced to broil a couple of steaks. I threw the heart and some ribs in the pot for a good stew later, and we ate the steaks and waited for the pot to boil. It was a good sign that Whiskey was able to eat at all.

"I think I could ride," she said abruptly. "If you could get me on my horse, we could make it into Caliope."

I nodded. "If we had horses, we probably could."

"They took the horses too?"

"Sure. They'll turn them loose somewhere, and they'll go back to Caliope when they're ready. And nobody's going to pay any attention or give a damn."

"Oh, my," she said, and I could see she was mighty close to tears. "You don't think they'd come back here, do you?"

"I kind of doubt it, if you mean the horses. They'd be back now if they were coming back."

"Will somebody look for us?"

I shrugged. "Who? I'd bet a big red sugar cookie that Sam and Red and Dutch are sitting in the Emporium right now drinking hot toddies. That rules out Jim. He's not going to go looking for us with them watching his every move."

"And that means we can't go to Caliope."

"It doesn't look like it. You'd never make it walking, and the snow's too deep for me to carry you. The best thing we can do is wait for a break in the weather and for you to get your strength back."

That evening she sat up, with a little help from me, and she ate some of the deer stew, which I'd doctored up with one of our three cans of tomatoes. I checked out her wound and it didn't look too bad, all things considered. It was clean, with no pus or gas or anything like that, and it seemed to me that it was healing. What was going on inside was anybody's guess, but rest and warm food wouldn't hurt. When you've got nothing better to lean on, common sense sometimes does the trick.

I thought about that and then I thought about Caliope, and the more I thought, the more I realized I had to go back. There was no other place to take Whiskey. I told her.

"I want to get you back to Caliope. I think Martha Hagen would hide you there, or maybe I could take you to Doc Myer, and he and his wife would keep you."

She nodded, as if she'd been thinking the same thing. "And what about you, Charlie?"

"I did some thinking today. I'm a little tired of all this running. Sooner or later I'm going to have to face Sam again, and it might as well be on my terms. I'm going to get our money back, one way or another. And I'm going to get the other two while I'm at it."

" 'Vengeance is mine, saith the Lord.' "

I shook my head. "Revenge is one thing, self-preservation's another. As long as they're alive, we're not safe. They tried to murder us, and they damned near succeeded. There's a law against that."

She nodded, satisfied. She hadn't needed much convincing. "I can help. I can handle that gun of mine pretty well."

Enough to kill a man? I thought, but I didn't say so. "We'll see what happens when the time comes."

"It may come sooner than you think, Charlie. I've been doing some thinking too. Once we get out of the valley here, it's pretty near all downhill to Caliope, isn't it?"

"Uh-huh."

"Well—why couldn't you make a sled and pull me?"

I tossed that one around in my mind for a bit. It wasn't impossible, of course. I could cut some saplings down in the creekbed and lash them together, and I was sure I could rig some kind of harness with our belts.

"What do you say?"

106

"It doesn't sound too bad," I admitted. "I'll get down to the creek tomorrow and see what I can find in the way of wood. Too bad we don't have some barrel staves. We could make a toboggan."

"You can't have everything." She smiled through her pain. "You're turning out to be a good man in a pinch, Charlie."

It was about the nicest thing anybody'd ever said to me, and I kept it in mind while I waited to fall asleep that night.

But our luck changed the next morning. I found the horses just outside. They were gaunted, but I guessed with a little rest they'd be able to make it into Caliope. I led them down to the creek and cut some young branches and stripped down some bark for them to feed on, and they ate it almost as if they'd been Indian horses. I left the saddles hanging from a limb out of the snow, and then I went back to the dugout to tell Whiskey the good news.

I was still of two minds about our leaving. On the one hand, the quicker I got her to a warm bed with good food and medical care, the faster she'd recover. But on the other hand, the ride into Caliope could kill her. All it would take would be her horse stumbling, and then the wound would reopen, and all the good of the past day or so would be undone. I wasn't doing too bad a job of taking care of her here, where it was warm and safe from the wind. But supposing something happened on the trip to Caliope? We'd be caught out in the open without shelter.

"If you're worried about me, Charlie, don't," Whiskey said. "I can make it fine."

"How will you mount?"

"You can pick me up and step up on the chopping block outside and put me in the saddle. I won't have to use my arms much at all."

I agreed to try it. "But if it hurts you any," I warned her, "we're going to hold off. Fair enough?"

"Fair enough."

I estimated the ride at three hours, considering the snow, and I wanted to hit town after dark. It's one thing to ride in on a pack of thieves, and it's another thing entirely to announce your arrival. The only chance I had of taking them was to surprise them.

Along about four o'clock, according to my watch, which never did run too well, I went down to the creek and saddled the horses and led them up to the dugout. I packed the best parts of the meat from the buck in the hide, and I made Whiskey eat what she could of the rest of the stew before we started. Good food never hurt any invalid, and it's always been my contention that hospitals starve the hell out of their patients.

I got Whiskey on her horse without too much trouble, and she didn't complain a bit. I guessed I'd watch her for a mile or so, and if she seemed to be handling it, then we'd go the rest of the way. There wasn't too much I could do about her wound, but I strapped her chest fairly tight to hold ribs and things in place, and I figured that ought to do it if anything would.

We stopped a couple of times to rest the horses, and once I found a big rock alongside the trail so I could lift her off and let her lie down on a blanket, but even so we fetched Caliope around eight. I took a little while to look the situation over from the ridge, and then we went on down to Doc Meyer's back door and I hammered on it until Mrs. Meyer came to see what the commotion was.

"Doc's tired," she said without any greeting.

"This lady's been shot through the chest and she needs help." I led Whiskey's horse up to the stoop and lifted her off, and she leaned against me.

"Oh, my goodness," Mrs. Meyer said. "In that case, come on in."

Doc came into his office and I helped him undress Whiskey. He looked at the wounds and pronounced them satisfactory. "There's not a lot I can do," he said. "Put on clean dressings and let nature take its course."

I blessed him silently for that. I don't have much use for doctors who mess around when they shouldn't. "There's another thing, Doc."

He brushed lanky white hair away from his forehead and gave me a piercing look out of his blue eyes, still unfaded at sixty. "This means trouble, I take it?" he asked politely.

"Yes," I said simply. And then I told him the whole story.

"No problem here," he said when I'd finished. "She can stay until she's better. It wouldn't be good sense to turn her out where they can take another shot at her, would it?"

I grinned my thanks. "If I can leave her here then, I'll be much obliged. I've got some business to take care of."

"The marshal?"

I nodded. "I've got to see him and swear out a warrant."

"He won't do anything, Charlie. He's up against something too big for him to handle."

"I've got to try it the legal way first, Doc. Maybe I can help him serve it, and that'll give him some guts."

"Chances are, you'll do what has to be done your own self," he sniffed. "I don't recollect he came out and helped you the time Pete Moffatt beat the stuffings out of you."

"I've still got to try it, Doc. I need every edge I can get."

14

I left Whiskey's horse tied up in back, in Doc's shed, and then I rode down to the back of the jail and pounded on the back door until Tom Scott came out to see who was breaking in or out, as the case might be.

"Look what the cat drug in," he said sourly. "Come on in, if you don't want to freeze your tail off out there."

"That's what I had in mind," I told him. "I want to swear out a warrant."

"For what?"

"Attempted murder of Whiskey and me."

"Against who?"

"Sam Bonner, Red James, and Dutch Evarts."

He looked tired, and when he spoke his voice was even more weary. "You better tell me all about it," he said, and I told him.

When I was done, he fished in the desk drawer for his bottle. He even thought to offer me a snort. "Now then, you're a mite late. The three gentlemen you mentioned rode out about three o'clock and said they weren't coming back. They had three bottles of rye whiskey, courtesy of Jim Hagen, new clothes, courtesy of Sol Levitan, and some nice fixings, courtesy of Bill Pearse. All gifts, of course."

"Oh, hell!"

"Well, every cloud has a silver lining, like they say. The town's well rid of them at any cost."

"For how long? And how many other shootists are going to hear about the easy pickings in Caliope?"

"I wouldn't know," he said sourly, and he took another nip at his bottle. This time he didn't pass it across the desk.

"All right, Tom. I want to swear out that warrant anyway. And then I want you to swear me in as a deputy."

"Hell, Charlie! You don't have jurisdiction outside of this town. And the place to get a warrant sworn out is up in Oberlin, where the sheriff'll do it. Until we get a county seat, he's the closest law there is. Unless you run into a U. S. marshal somewhere along the line."

"You can take my deposition and swear out a local warrant and deputize me. That's all I'll need."

"To chase down three armed men who already just missed killing you and your lady friend? You're crazy, Charlie."

"Crazy or not, I want it."

He threw up his hands in mock surrender, and then he reached for paper and a scratchy old pen. "All right, let's have the charges."

When I had the warrant safely folded in my pocket and a new tin star pinned on my coat, I left Tom Scott to meditate with the rest of his bottle, and then I took my horse and Whiskey's down to the livery stable and got a fresh horse from Joe Huntly, the hostler. I didn't know how far I was going to have to go before I caught up with Sam Bonner and his partners, but it never hurt anybody

112

to be prepared. After that I went to the Emporium to see Jim Hagen.

"They paid me every damn cent they owed," he told me. "I gave them three bottles of whiskey as a fare-you-well present, just to keep them off my back."

"How come they paid you when they didn't pay anybody else?"

He permitted himself a small grin, probably of satisfaction at having accomplished what the rest of the town couldn't. "I told them right at the start that they'd pay cash for their drinks if they wanted to gamble in here, and then I showed them my little persuader." He meant the sawed-off scattergun he kept under the bar. "That's the only kind of language they understand."

"I guess. Did you hear which way they were heading?"

He shrugged. "I heard a lot of talk, some of it from them, some of it from other people. If I was to bet money on it, I'd say Wallace. It's the closest railroad town, and that's the way they're apt to travel in winter. They're not real hardcases who can live out on the prairie for a couple, three months. They need the soft life." He looked at me. "Unless they're still hunting for you, that is."

"I doubt that. They think I'm coyote food by now." I told him the whole story.

His face grew white and pinched with anger as I talked, and at the end of it he said, "You came off lucky, Charlie. If I was you, I'd thank the Lord you didn't lose any more than your money, and that you and Whiskey are still alive."

"I've done just that, Jim. But I've got a warrant

for their arrest, and I'm going after them. Want to ride along?"

"I'm too old for that stuff, Charlie."

"Sure, Jim."

"I'm sorry. I wish I could go with you, but I just can't."

I knew what he meant. He wasn't going to stick his neck out and maybe get it chopped off. And when I thought about it, he was about the only real friend I had in Caliope. If he wouldn't help me, nobody would.

I thanked him and asked him to forget I'd been there and not to mention anything about me or Whiskey to anybody. He said he wouldn't, and I guess I could count on him for that much.

I stopped at the doctor's to see how Whiskey was doing, and Doc said she was sleeping. "That's about all we can hope for, Charlie. From now on, it's up to her constitution and God. If you're a praying man, it might not hurt to say a few."

"She looked pretty good when I brought her in."

"Sure she did, but that ride didn't do her a lot of good. She's going to need a lot of rest and a hell of a lot of luck. She's not out of the woods yet, by any stretch of the imagination."

That put a damper on things, but I was too busy figuring what I'd do next to worry about it.

There was starlight, as there usually is on a clear, cold night, and I didn't have too much trouble picking up the tracks of three horses in the snow outside town. They were following the stage route to Wallace, which was a tad longer than the one I'd used, but an easier trail to follow, since a stage couldn't go over some of the rough country a man on horseback could.

I followed the tracks for ten miles until they mingled with other tracks, but by that time I knew them by heart and I guessed it would only be a matter of time before they turned off and cut across country. Sure enough, in another five miles they slanted off to the southwest.

That much was good, but I could see clouds against the stars in front of me, and that could only mean more snow. That was good in that they'd have to stop and make camp long before they reached Wallace, but it was bad in that I'd no longer be able to follow tracks. Once I lost them, I'd have to guess and choose at where they were, and it was more than likely I'd have to go all the way to Wallace before I came across them.

I'd been traveling about four hours, I guessed, when I came upon a dark lump in the snow that shouldn't have been there. I stopped and hauled out my field glasses from the saddle bag and had me a look. It was a horse, and by the looks of him, he was dead or all but. I couldn't see a quiver from his legs, and he was all hunched down on his belly, his head lolled off to one side. I rode up to him slow and easy, watching for somebody hiding behind him, until I remembered that Sam would never dream of anybody trying to follow him.

There wasn't a lot I could tell from looking at the horse, except that he'd probably been ridden to death pushing through the snow. The saddle was still on him, but the saddlebags had been taken. I checked out the tracks around the dead horse and saw a lot of boot marks, like everybody'd dismounted to see what could be done, and then I saw one set of boot tracks following the other two horses. They'd probably decided to take turns riding the other two mounts, I guessed, and if they were as dumb as they seemed to be, they'd ride them to death too.

I'd had it pretty easy so far, just following tracks, because the others had had to break trail through maybe twelve inches of snow, and my horse only had to follow them to have a good beaten trail where he didn't have to work so hard. If Sam and his partners had been a little smarter and quicker, they'd have taken turns with the lead and ridden out in single file, where each horse would get a chance to rest up by following in a beaten track. Another way to have done it would have been to let the horses go ahead with everybody on foot, letting the horses break trail without carrying any weight. But these men had never spared horses in their lives, nor had they ever had to live in open country where you couldn't go to a livery stable and buy yourself another horse when the one you had dropped dead. That gave me a hell of an edge on them, but it still wasn't enough to even out the advantage three of them would have over one man.

Just about the time the snow began to fall again, I saw a pinprick of light downhill and over to the right of me, and I knew they'd stopped to make some kind of camp. Either that, or they'd left the man on foot behind to make it out the best way he could. I rode slowly toward the light until I was maybe half a mile away, and then I dismounted and led my horse off to the side so I could sneak up to the camp on foot and see what I was up against. A little farther on, the ground dropped off pretty suddenly, and I knew where I was. I'd come down to one of the little creeks that feeds the Smoky Hill River, and that's where they were camped, down in the timber and close to water and fallen wood for a fire.

I tied the horse to a tree, took out the Sharps and checked to make sure it was loaded, and then I stalked from tree to tree until I could see the fire. It was a pretty big one, bigger than it needed to be, especially when you never knew but what a stray Indian or two might be roaming around looking for a scalp to add to his collection or a horse to borrow.

The three of them were sitting by the fire, not lying down to rest like sensible men, and not even keeping any kind of watch. I guessed I'd have to wait until they decided to go to sleep and then try to get to them and disarm them, which would be a tricky business at best.

But it didn't work out that way. I could hear voices, although I couldn't hear what they were saying. It sounded to me like they were arguing, maybe about whether they were going to leave one man behind or about who was going to take the first watch. I slid down behind a fallen tree and trained my rifle over it to cover them, and I waited. From time to time the snow came down in a burst as a tree let go of its load, and then I couldn't see them at all, but mostly I could see them pretty plain, even if I couldn't hear them.

Finally one of them got up and went a little way off, as if he had to relieve himself, and suddenly little fireflies danced from one of the other men, and the flat slap-slap-slap of three revolver shots came clearly across the distance. The man who had gone a little apart fell forward in the snow and lay still. The man who'd fired went over to him and turned him over with his boot, and then the other man stood up and went over and stood beside him.

That was one way of solving the problem of who was going to ride the horses and who was going to walk, I thought, but having never killed a man in my life, I was kind of sick about it. In Sam's world life was cheaper than a frazzled deuce of diamonds, but I still counted anybody's life as worth something, and I couldn't see killing a man for something as worthless as money. I had to get hold of myself and make up my mind that I was operating in Sam's world now, and that my standards, whatever they might be, didn't hold worth a hoot.

Of course life would have been a lot simpler if I'd been like Sam; I could have picked them off one by one from where I was, and I'd have gotten two of them before the third one could get mounted. But I wasn't sorry I was different. True enough, I was tracking them, and I was going to get my money back, but if it had only been the money I could have let it go. It was Whiskey being shot and my life being at risk as long as Sam Bonner went unpunished. The money came third.

The two who were left picked up a couple of saddlebags and shook them out in the snow. They must have found what they were looking for pretty quickly, because they came back to the fire and started counting money, the way it looked. I trained my field glasses on them, and sure enough, that's what they were doing. One of them was Sam Bonner and the other was the man I'd kicked off the train, Dutch Evarts. Unless they'd done some quick substituting, the dead man had to be Red James. I wondered if he'd been any relation to Jesse and decided not; no relative of Jesse James would have been stupid enough to turn his back on a couple of cutthroats like Dutch and Sam.

I kept waiting for them to go to sleep so I could come in and disarm them, but they just sat there at the fire and talked, and after a while it stopped snowing and they got up and started to monkey with their saddles. Now I had to figure on taking them while they were awake, and that didn't make me too happy. I watched them saddle up, figuring on taking them before they got mounted, when my horse nickered in the dark woods behind me.

Sam reacted almost immediately by jumping into the saddle. The other man, Dutch, was the one I had in my sights, but when I jerked off my shot, it went past Dutch and hit the horse. The big Sharps boomed like a cannon, and the horse that had been hit dropped like a sack of wet feed. Dutch was fast enough getting behind the horse and snapping a couple of shots from a revolver in my general direction while Sam skedaddled. There was no point in hanging around and letting Sam come up on me from behind or finding my horse, so I shoved a new shell in the chamber of the Sharps and trotted back toward where I'd left my mount. I got there maybe five minutes later and hunkered down alongside him, waiting to see what Sam was going to do.

For a time there was no movement at all, and when I heard it, it was back toward the campfire. Score one for Sam: he was too smart to go chasing a horse tied up in the timber when all he had to do

119

was back off to cover and call Dutch to bring the saddlebags and come over to him. Once they were away from the fire, they could head out riding double and lose themselves in the timber. With luck, they'd have enough of a head start to set up an ambush. I'd had the advantage of surprise, and all it had bought me was one dead horse and two shootists who knew I was out there waiting for them.

There was only one thing to do, get to higher ground where I could see what was going on. Down here in the timber, it would be too easy for them to stalk me, if that was what they had in mind, or to make tracks out of there and take advantage of some high ground themselves.

15

Somewhere along the line it dawned on me that I was in danger of being hunted down. Now they needed my horse, if they were going to get to Wallace ahead of me. And since I was on the horse, that meant I was fair game. The only good thing I could see was that they only had one horse and I could keep away from them if I saw them coming.

I picked a spot where two hills overlapped somewhat, and I dismounted and waited for something to happen. It was quiet enough, the way it generally is on a cold night, and the stars began to fade before I saw movement at the edge of the timber, and then it was a long way off. At a guess they'd been crawling around in the woods looking for me, hoping to get hold of my horse and leave me on foot or dead. Now they were shooting for second best, trying to get out of the area before I saw them.

I led the horse below the skyline and rode out on a course that would intercept them when they crossed the low hills on the south bank of the river. When I got the field glasses on them, they were plodding along, both of them on the one horse and that looking like it was ready to drop. I never had much use for anybody who could mistreat an animal under any circumstances, and I had even less use for this pair.

At one point they were five hundred yards away, and it would have been easy enough to pick one of them off or at least drop the horse, but I held back. The way Sam had handled Red James indicated that he would take care of Dutch for me too, sooner or later, and it was a point of honor with me to turn him over to Tom Scott, if only to prove that I could do what the marshal hadn't been able to do. There was always the horse, but I didn't much like the idea of shooting the horse if I could help it, partly because the horse hadn't done anything to me, and partly because I'd be stuck with two prisoners on foot.

It was full light now, or as light as it was apt to get. Dawn had come only as a lightening of the grayness in the east, and my senses told me there would be more snow. I guessed I had no choice but to take the horse and let them do some walking, and I lined up the sights on the animal's forequarter and started to take a lead. And then the horse dropped. It just up and quit, without my having to fire a shot. The two of them jumped clear and stood there arguing about what to do next. Dutch could consider himself lucky, I thought. Now there was no reason for Sam to shoot him, other than the obvious one that Sam would then get all the money. But right now Sam would figure that he needed that extra gun more than he needed the money. That would keep.

There was nothing to be gained by shooting over

their heads and hollering for them to throw down their guns until I knew what they had in mind. By my reckoning, it was another thirty miles to Wallace, maybe twenty-five back to Caliope. If I had been in their boots, I would have cut my losses by getting back into the timber and taking my chances with the lone sharpshooter. But then, I wasn't Sam.

After a while, they decided to get the horse on its feet. Even those two were smart enough to know that the horse wasn't going any place with two of them aboard, so they started to lead it back toward the river and the timber. I could see they were carrying rifles or carbines, whichever, and I decided they weren't as dumb as they looked. They at least had sense enough to know that they couldn't make it to Wallace until the horse was rested. If they had to, they could survive in the timber along the river, provided they had food.

I'd picked up a good supply of jerky before I left, so I was in fairly good shape, outside of being worn to a frazzle from all that riding last night and yesterday afternoon. I could wait them out or follow them, one or the other, depending upon what they did next. If they had food, they'd stay in the river bottom and try to hunt me down and get my horse. If they didn't, they might figure they'd do better heading for Caliope and getting a fresh start on fresh mounts.

I watched them carefully until they re-entered the woods and were lost to sight, and then I waited a little longer and fought a battle with sleep by chewing a strip of jerky and telling myself I had to make it back to be with Whiskey.

Sleep won for a little while, maybe half an hour, and then the cold woke me and I scanned the timber for some sign of smoke or movement. There was none, and that bothered me. I'd lost them, because I couldn't see them. Even now they might be searching for my trail and coming up behind me. It didn't bother me too much, because my horse was fresher. They'd never catch me, not both of them together on that poor, sad horse, and not even one of them riding it could come close.

After a while I decided that the thing to do was check out the possible ways they could go, and that's when I saw them again. They had moved through the timber and come out the other side, and they were following the trail they'd made coming in, both of them walking now and leading the horse. I let them go over a hill and get out of sight, and then I mounted and retraced my trail to the river. I could stay behind them and herd them into Caliope, if things worked out that way. I kind of hoped they would, because it would save me the trouble of guarding them all the way in.

Again I wondered why they hadn't taken time to rest and maybe make a fire. They must have known there was only one of me, because if there'd been more, they'd be prisoners or dead by now. And unless they had food to keep them going, the timber and its cottontail population was their only hope of making it.

Snow began to fall by the time I fetched the woods, but it was only powder snow, nothing to be worried about unless it got worse. I stopped for a bit and cut some branches and stripped some bark for the horse, and then I led it through the fallen timber, around big walnut and elm and cottonwood trees to the other side. On the way I passed their camp in a little stand of cedar, and I saw Red James's body lying beside a tree where he'd fallen. I stopped for a moment to check him out and take his revolver, just in case I might want a hideaway gun. I stuck it down my boot leg and went on.

It was easy enough to follow the fresh trail Sam and Dutch were making, especially since the snow hadn't covered the original trail they'd made coming in. I caught up with them fifteen minutes later; they were plodding along up the slope of a little hill I remembered coming over last night, just before the snow, and I stopped and held position well back of them until they were beyond the next hill.

I don't know how long it took me to figure out that Sam wasn't as dumb as I'd figured him to be. Maybe half an hour, maybe more. Whatever, old Sam knew what he was doing. He wasn't resting anybody, including himself, because he wasn't going back to Caliope. He was going to hit the stage road down to Monument, more than likely, and catch a stage southbound to the Kansas Pacific. I'd figured him to be drawing to an inside straight, and all along he'd had three-of-a-kind.

I poked along in back of them, staying just close enough to keep them in sight, and sometimes I got off and walked too, partly to save the horse and partly to keep from falling asleep. I didn't have too much to worry about until they fetched up on the stage road. After that I'd have to take them, if I could. It was nice to know I could put it off for a

125

while, since it was something I didn't particularly feel like doing.

The snow tapered off after a bit and a little break in the clouds let the sun through, enough so I could see grass stems above the snow where the wind had swept it. I crested a rise and saw them headed up the next one, staggering along like a couple of drunks and pulling the horse along. It was time.

I stayed far enough back for the Sharps to give me an edge with its long range, and then I threw a round in the snow ahead of them. They both whirled around, and I yelled for them to drop their guns. One of them, probably Sam, snapped off a shot with a carbine, but it missed me by a good ten yards. The other one took off scrambling up the hill as I pushed a fresh shell into the breech. This time I aimed carefully and low and shot him in the leg. I still couldn't bring myself to kill a man, even though he'd probably shot either me or Whiskey. He went down in the snow, rolling over backward, and then he was still.

The shooter pumped four rounds toward me, but he was still wild. I pulled back the hammer on the Sharps and aimed for his right arm, but I hit the rifle instead. It went sailing into the snow. I fished for another cartridge, aimed again, and found him in my sights. But he had his hands up now, and he was yelling something I couldn't understand, the wind being at my back.

When I was a hundred yards away, I told him to throw out his revolver. Now I could see that it was Sam, and I figured I had it made. There are damn few men good enough to plug a man with a revolver

126

at a hundred yards, and the boom of the big Fifty had probably convinced him that I could sit out of range of any of his weapons and drill a hole in him any time I wanted.

The revolver went sailing into the snow along with the rifle, and I told him to turn around and face the other way. I'd learned that trick from an old sheriff up in Wyoming Territory. "Never let the man see what you're doing," he'd told me. He'd also showed me how to search a man so he couldn't take you, and it was lucky I remembered, because when I started to search Sam, he tried to kick me in the groin. That's about all a man can do, when you've got a gun on him and you're close enough to search him, but even that won't work if you know what you're doing. I had my left leg inside his and my left hand in the small of his back, and the minute he made his move, I kicked his left leg out from under him and pushed him face-down in the snow. He lost his wind with a whoosh, and then it was easy. As I'd expected, I found another gun on him, a sawed-down Navy Colt in the back of his belt. I tucked that away in my coat for future reference, and then I got a rawhide thong out of my pocket and lashed his hands behind him. I wasn't too worried about his feet, because he had no place to go.

I'd almost forgotten about Dutch Evarts, and that was a mistake because when I turned to where he'd been, he wasn't there. He must have managed to crawl over the hill.

I told Sam to start walking, and then I got the reins of the horses in my left hand and moved in close behind him. "You're going over the hill first,"

I told him.

He told me what he thought of me, but it came out a little cockeyed, his mouth being sore where he'd hit. I let him get to the top of the hill and nothing happened, so I came up a little to the side and Dutch threw a round at me that came so close I could feel the wind of it. He started to lever another round into his rifle, but I held the Sharps on him and yelled, "Don't!" He looked down that big bore and changed his mind.

Sam stood there like a cigar-store Indian, not making a move to help his partner the way I'd have expected him to do. I held the gun on Dutch and told him to throw away the rifle and drop his gun belt, and he yelled back that he couldn't stand, that I'd half shot his leg off. It was a lie, because there was no blood in his tracks. I guessed I'd aimed for his leg and got his boot heel.

I got out another thong and put the Sharps in the saddle boot and took out Sam's hideaway gun, watching the two of them right along. Then I had Dutch lie on his face in the snow, and just for good measure had Sam follow suit. When they were both down and safely apart, I tied Dutch's hands together and searched him thoroughly, coming up with a bowie knife and a set of knuckle-dusters. Nice fellow, Dutch.

I set them to walking and followed at a safe distance, leading the horse they'd pretty near killed, and congratulating myself. I had them both in custody and I hadn't had to shoot anybody doing it.

We humped along to the stage road, and it was plain to see that there hadn't been a stage through from either direction since the storm. There had been a couple of riders, but the wind was covering their tracks. I guessed we had about ten miles to go, which wouldn't have been much if we'd all been fresh. But however much sleep the other two had gotten, I hadn't had enough to keep a jay-bird going, and I was beginning to feel it. I waited until I found a low place where the stage road crossed a draw, and then I picked a couple of trees that looked good, in that they were too big to pull up and far enough apart so my two prisoners couldn't do much more than talk. I took Dutch's belt off and sidestepped when he tried to kick me, and then I told him to sit down with his back to the tree. He said he wouldn't, he was damned if he was going to take orders from a damned cardplayer. I said that was all right with me, and then I laid the barrel of the Starr alongside his head, none too gently, and he went right down, pretty as you please.

"Now what are you going to do?" Sam grinned. "We're going to get you, sonny, one way or another. We can wait."

I didn't answer him. Instead, I ran Dutch's belt through his arms above the elbows, dragged him to his tree, and cinched the belt around it. Then I looked at Sam and grinned. "Want to sit down quietly? Or do you want a headache?"

The handsome bastard gave me back my grin. "Quietly, by all means. I don't trust you with a gun, sonny."

He obligingly sat down next to his tree, and I secured him the same way I had Dutch. And then I picked a tree apart where I could watch the two of them without their being able to see me, leaned against it, and promptly fell asleep.

I managed about two hours before the cold woke me up, and it was high time. Dutch had managed to put the time to good use, and he was scissoring his bound arms loose from the belt. Sam was imitating him, and it was only a matter of minutes before the two of them would be working on the rawhide thongs girding their arms.

When Dutch got his arms out of the belt and stood up, he leaned against his tree, still shaky. "Getting yours, Sam?"

"Getting it," Sam grunted. "Shut up before he hears you and wakes up."

I took out Sam's hideaway gun and came up behind Dutch as quietly as I could. Then I laid the cold barrel against the back of his neck. "Thanks for saving me the trouble, Dutch. Now we can help Sam out of his predicament and get moving."

Sam spat in the snow and said nothing, but I could feel his hate like a burning brand. If he ever got the chance, he'd kill me by slow degrees, just to watch me squirm.

I felt the hate all the rest of the way to Caliope, and it made me realize how close I'd come to being bushwhacked, once they got loose. So far, I'd been luckier than any man has a right to count on. Not smart, just lucky. There's a difference, and some men make a mistake between the two, because they want to think they're a tad smarter than the average run of people. It was a mistake I'd almost made, but the sight of Dutch within moments of getting himself free to hit me over the head had knocked some of the conceit out of me. In fact it had purely scared the hell out of me, and I stayed scared until Tom Scott locked the two of them in the back cell of the jail.

16

"I can't say as I'm happy to see you," Tom Scott grumbled. "You could have taken the two of them and lost them somewhere down the line."

"You're welcome, for what it's worth," I told him. "Now if you think you can keep them locked up, I'm going to catch some sleep."

I left the marshal grumbling about his new responsibilities and walked down the street to Doc Meyer's house to see how Whiskey was faring.

Doc was noncommittal. "She's about the same," he said gravely. "She hasn't lost any ground, but she hasn't gained any either. I'd say another twenty-four hours will tell the tale."

"Is there anything she needs I can get for her?"

"Not a thing," he said. "Get some sleep and maybe you can see her in the morning. She's been in a coma ever since you left, but I'm thinking she might snap out of it, once she gets rested up a little."

I stopped at Jim Hagen's saloon to tell him the news, and he wagged his head and chuckled. "I can't believe you took on the two of them," he said. "Boy, they are one hell of a pair to tangle with. You were lucky they took care of the red-head for you."

"It took a hell of a lot of luck, Jim," I said, remembering how close I'd come to being bushwhacked.

"Everybody needs luck, no matter how good he is. Hickok was the fastest man with a gun I ever seen, and it didn't make a damn bit of difference when his luck run out."

"I guess. I'm going to head for Mrs. Durning's and get some sleep."

"Want a drink before you go?"

"Nope. One drink would put me under the table right now. I want to get some sleep and go see Whiskey in the morning. That's about all the ambition I've got right now."

Mrs. Durning gave me my old room with no questions asked, and I slept until ten the next morning.

When I came downstairs, I was wearing clean clothes, courtesy of Mrs. Durning's midnight efforts, and I had managed a hot bath in her kitchen. Life was looking up.

I got on the outside of a platter of eggs and sausage and pancakes and three cups of strong coffee, and then I went out to meet the world. It was a bright cold day, and a bitter little wind crept around the corners of buildings and stirred the surface of the snow. My first stop was Bill's store. It was time we got something settled.

Bill was friendly, unusually so. "You're some kind of local hero," he said. "The entire community is grateful to you for bringing those ruffians to justice."

"Bill, you're going to be a shoe-in as a politician. You can change sides faster than a flea can change dogs."

"What in the devil do you mean by that?"

I looked around the store in which I'd once clerked, savoring the good smells of oiled harness and greased steel from the hardware section. "I mean you and the rest of the town put up with them for quite a while. You let them run rough-shod all over you, and you didn't say a word. You let them come in here hunting me, and you did nothing. And now you're all in favor of having them in jail."

"You've got it all wrong, Charlie. We were terrified by them. They substituted their guns for the law, and we had nothing to stop them. Tom Scott never did a thing, never lifted a hand. A fine excuse for a marshal he turned out to be."

I helped myself to a cigar from the glass jar on the counter. "Tom Scott is no better than the town he serves. He can't be. He knew you wouldn't back him, so he did nothing."

"That's not what this town expects of a marshal. Maybe you ought to consider the position."

I grinned and blew out a cloud of smoke. "For thirty dollars a month, I'm not about to risk my life to protect this town or any other. You people don't deserve a good lawman."

"That's not fair. We have one of the finest communities in western Kansas. Look at our streets, look at our homes."

"Look at the way you let Pete Moffatt do what he pleases. Look at the money a few of you are making at the expense of the rest. If there weren't profit in taking in unsavory characters, you might be law-abiding, and then you'd deserve a good lawman. But you turn your face the other way if the lawbreaker has money to spend. You just made a little mistake with Sam Bonner and his gang—they had money, but they didn't want to spend it."

He got busy with a ledger. "There's no talking to you," he said. "You're a sorehead and a troublemaker."

I leaned over the counter and planted a hand on the ledger. "Bill? You want to tell me how those men happened to come here from Wallace? Or do you want to let me guess?"

"I don't know what you mean," he said, but his face reddened. "I'm busy. I have work to do."

Doc Meyer wouldn't let me up to see Whiskey. "It wouldn't do you any good," he said. "She's still unconscious. Just let nature take its course."

I told him I'd stop back in a couple of hours to see if there'd been a change, and then I went on down to the jail to see what Tom Scott was up to.

"Glad you stopped by," he said. "Your friends in there have been bitching all night long about how you bushwhacked them."

"They didn't happen to mention how they shot Red James in the back because they didn't want to split my money three ways, did they?"

He chuckled. "Can't say as they did. Charlie? How's about you sitting down here and keeping an eye on things while I go get me some breakfast and a shave and a clean shirt?"

I had nothing better to do, so I told him I'd oblige. "Just get back in a couple of hours so I can stop by Doc's and find out how Whiskey's getting along."

He promised he would, and then he left me to enjoy the hospitality of a hot stove, coffee that was half lye, and a Wichita newspaper from last month. The marshal was no great reader.

Sam and Dutch were asleep or pretending to be, so I hunted up some rags and cleaned Sam's hideaway gun, the one I'd recovered from Red James, and my Starr and reloaded them, borrowing cartridges for the Colts from the marshal's cupboard.

The armament wasn't too shabby for a town that size. Scott had two sawed-off double-barrel shotguns, three Spencer rifles, and a fairly new Winchester. In the drawer of his desk were four new-model Colt forty-fives, and that wasn't counting the one he was wearing. I guessed he could fit out three or four deputies with no problem, if he could find them. Given Caliope, it was unlikely that he would.

I passed over the office bottle, which was only half-full anyhow, and went on exploring. There were little packets of papers, each tied carefully with cord and superscribed with a name. Some were familiar, others were not. I put them back in the drawer and closed it. I wasn't interested in nosing about other people's business, having enough of my own to take care of.

A sound from the cell in back roused me, and I turned around to see Sam Bonner working away with a piece of wire, trying to pick the lock of his cell. It didn't look like much of a lock to pick, but then he couldn't see what he was doing, the lock being on the outside of the door and Sam being on the inside.

I let him get a good start with the wire, and then I came over and slapped his hand away and got the wire out. "My, my," I said. "You're kind of tricky, Sam."

He spat on the floor and turned away. "That won't stop me from getting out, sonny," he growled. "You just wait around, and you'll see what happens to you."

"Sure, Sam."

136

I went back to the desk and tossed the wire in a drawer. Then I helped myself to the coffee and waited for Tom Scott. I split my time between wondering how a man as good-looking as Sam Bonner could be as big a scoundrel as he was, and worrying about Whiskey.

All the while I'd been chasing Sam and his partners I'd been pretty cocky about Whiskey. She was young and strong, she'd pull through. But now that I had time on my hands, I started to worry in earnest. A slug through the chest was no laughing matter. More often than not, the recipient dies. The only thing I could think of that was at all hopeful was that the slug probably had come out of a .36 Colt, because that was what both Sam and Dutch carried. A .44 would have torn her up so bad inside, she wouldn't have made it through the first night.

Tom came back in time to rescue the rest of his coffee. "Have any trouble with them?" he asked.

"Nope. Handsome tried to pick the lock with a piece of wire, but I took it away from him."

The marshal nodded. "Last feller tried that bunged up the lock so bad he had to stay over an extra day until the gunsmith could take time to come and take the lock apart. Maybe Bonner did the same."

"Fat chance," Sam called. "You won't keep me in here long."

"Long enough," Tom Scott said.

"For what?"

"For the circuit judge to get here and try your case." Tom Scott turned to me. "That's going to be quite a while, the way it looks. A rider come through from Platte Bridge this morning and said the stages aren't running. There's heavy snow up north of here,

137

and there ain't nothing getting through."

"I'm not going anyplace anyway," I told him.

"For sure you're not. You got to stay and testify."

"My pleasure. How soon do you think the judge can get here?"

"Oh, hell, he's not due here for another two weeks. And that's not counting in the weather."

Somehow I had thought things would move a little faster than that. I only had the foggiest notion of how the law worked, never having been acquainted with it on either side until now, but it seemed to me that if things worked out the way they should, Whiskey would get better and Sam and Dutch would get the short end of a long rope. After that, Whiskey and I would find us a preacher and get hitched and start raising kids and cattle on the old Picken claim. Now, it might take a month before justice was done, as they always said in the Deadwood Dick stories I'd read.

I left Tom Scott to the rest of his coffee and walked down the street to Sol Levitan's, where I bought a pretty little music box that played "O Promise Me" for Whiskey. It seemed like a good idea; she could lie in bed recovering and listen to the tinkle-tinkle of the music box, and it would remind her that we were going to make things official-like one of these days.

Sol was glad to see me, as always. "It is a good thing you put those men behind bars," he said. "If you ever need help with anything, let me know, Charlie."

"You'll be about the first I'll ask, Sol," I promised him.

He grinned slyly and pulled out a sawed-off double-barrel with the stock cut down as well. "This time

I'm ready for them."

"Them" were already behind bars, but it was good to know Sol was taking some active measures. I was glad to know too that he was smart enough to know his own limitations. You don't have to be any kind of shot to pulverize an opponent with a sawed-off, provided he's obliging enough to stand no more than fifteen feet from you.

I took the music box and walked on to Doc Meyer's, and this time Doc said I could go up and see Whiskey. "She's conscious and she took some hot soup," he told me. "But don't go to getting her excited. She is still a mighty sick young woman. You can talk to her for maybe ten minutes, and then I want you out of here so she can get her rest."

I agreed and went up the stairs to the room where Whiskey was recuperating.

Her face was all sharp and drawn, and her hair was kind of plastered to her head. Only her eyes were warm and alive, and when she spoke it came out very soft and far away. "I knew you'd be back, Charlie," she said. "I always knew you'd do it."

"They told you about Sam and Dutch?"

She nodded. "Mrs. Meyer told me."

I handed her the music box, having wound it up on my way up the stairs. "You just push this little lever, and then it plays. I figured it would give you something to listen to." I started it going, and it tinkled away at a good clip.

"It's real pretty, Charlie," she whispered. "I've been thinking about the good times we had together, you know? I'm glad we didn't wait around for a preacher."

"That's the next thing on the agenda," I told her.

"As soon as you get well, we're going to find us a preacher and get hitched, and then we'll build a nice little house out there on the claim. We can be out there by Christmas."

She nodded as if she agreed, but then she said, "Charlie? If I don't make it, promise me you won't waste your life mooning around about me. I don't want to spoil all your good years."

"Don't talk that kind of nonsense, honey. You're going to get well and we're going to have one hell of a good life together."

"All right," she said. "I'll be cheerful. And you be cheerful too, you hear?"

I promised her I would, and then Mrs. Meyer came up to say it was time I left and let Whiskey get some rest.

I went back to the saloon, where I'd started, and Jim said if I didn't have anything better in mind, I might want to deal some poker later on. "No stage passengers in, of course, but there's some locals said they'd like to sit in on a few hands with you."

I agreed to it, and I went on to Mrs. Durning's in time to change my shirt and clean the Sharps and slide it under the covers, just in case somebody took a notion to acquire it while I was out. Then I went down to dinner, which was fried chicken and snap beans and mounds of mashed potatoes to take care of all that good gravy.

I thought a little about what Whiskey had said, but I told myself that all sick people thought they were going to die, that it was natural for her to feel that way at times, and then I felt better.

Four players came around to the Emporium about three in the afternoon, and I guessed the cold weather had kept business down to a minimum, which gave them time to play. Jim Hagen set a bottle of rye whiskey on the table along with five glasses, and I put a dollar in to pay for my share. That was pretty generous, since the whiskey only cost two dollars a bottle, and since I wasn't gong to be drinking much of it anyhow. But I figured I'd make back the dollar pretty quick once the game started, and it created good will, like the merchants are always saying.

Everybody wanted to play five-card stud, which is a good game. The easy part of it is, you can see a lot of exposed cards if everybody stays with the bettor. Counting yourself, you can see twenty open cards, which leaves thirty-two blind ones. If you can see four aces open, you know nobody's going to have a pair of aces. If you can see two kings and you know you've got two, you're probably high man on a pair. They can beat you with three or four of a kind, and you can check the open cards and rule out a few players right from the start. Then you have to figure your odds against what's showing and what's left. It sounds more complicated than it really is, and a smart player can pretty much size up the worth of his hand before the heavy betting starts.

I wasn't playing for blood, and nobody else was either. I had a drink in front of me, and from time to time I sipped at it, but I let the others go ahead and have themselves a good time. I deliberately bet on a couple of losing hands just to show I wasn't out for a killing, and then I settled down to play good poker, betting heavy when I had people sticking with me, but never making more than four or five dollars on a hand. I lost some too, because even the best of players is going to lose a few, but by five o'clock I was

141

twenty dollars ahead. Best of all, nobody was mad about it. Dick Evans, the banker, broke up the game finally, saying it was about time he went home to supper. He had a paunch with a gold watch chain over it, just like you'd expect a banker to have, and he patted his paunch when he talked about supper.

I let them file out, and then I went over to the bar and gave Jim the two dollars that was coming to him. "Anything lined up for tonight?"

He shook his head. "Not that I know of. Just what might happen by."

It was about time to go back to Mrs. Durning's and get supper, and I was about to say so when I saw the expression on Jim's face change.

"I've been waiting for you to finish up," Pete Moffatt said. "It's about time we had that little talk of ours, hero."

He was drunk as a skunk, but that doesn't matter much to some men. When it comes to fighting, they can be twice as fast and twice as mean drunk as they are sober. Worst of all, he had a gun in his hand, and there are very few men can draw against an exposed weapon and live. I didn't figure it was worthwhile to try to be one of them, so I shrugged and tried not to show I was scared out of my wits and said, "Want a drink?"

"Hell, no. I don't want to drink with you."

"Suit yourself. Jim, you want to pour me one?"

It was a bid for time, something to distract him, and Jim took his time about pouring the drink and pushing it toward me. I fished out a quarter and put it on the bar, and I tried to figure out how I could get the Starr out of my holster without Pete noticing and spilling my guts all over the floor.

But that wasn't what he had in mind. "Take off that gunbelt," he ordered. "Me and you are going outside so's our little talk don't spoil Jim's furniture. You go out there first, and don't try to run away, or I'll have to shoot you and that'll spoil the fun."

I dropped the gunbelt, thinking all the while that things hadn't changed a hell of a lot. True, I was younger and smarter, but that didn't cut down Pete's size any. He was still close to six feet tall, he was still two hundred pounds, and he didn't look as if the years of drinking and brooding on what he figured was a disgrace to the family name and murder had changed him any for the better. If I was lucky, I was going to have one lick at him, and that was all.

I got out in the street with a little light coming out of the Emporium and a cold wind tickling the surface of the snow, and I turned around quickly to see Pete coming out of the saloon with killing in mind. His gun was still in his hand, and he hadn't made any move to drop his gunbelt.

"Going to drop the gun, Pete?" I asked him. "Or are you going to try your hand at shooting an unarmed man?"

He gave me a mean grin and told me something about my ancestors. It wasn't complimentary. "I want you on your knees, boy. I want to hear you tell me how you killed my little girl. And then I'm going to send you off to hell, where you belong."

I knew that if I got down on my knees he'd have me where he wanted me. There would be no way I could take him. "You're too drunk to fight, Pete," I told him. "Maybe you're too drunk to shoot too."

The bullet threw up snow by my right foot almost before I saw the gunflash and heard the report. "Get down, Charlie! I want to hear it!"

And then the door of the saloon opened and Jim Hagen said, "Put it down, Pete, before I let some daylight in you." Jim was standing there in his shirtsleeves, his sawed-off in his hands. At four feet, he couldn't very well miss.

"Stay out of this, Jim!" Pete roared. "This here's a private discussion."

"Not the way you rigged it. You want a fistfight, that's one thing. You want to shoot a man, that's another matter. I don't want to see you commit murder."

For answer, Pete raised the gun, and then Jim slammed the barrels of the sawed-off alongside his head and Pete went down all in a heap. I stepped forward and picked up Pete's gun and stuck it in my belt. "I owe you one, Jim," I said, and it didn't even sound like my voice.

"Don't mention it. I generally don't interfere with private affairs, but I couldn't let him shoot you down. If it was going to be a fair fight, that was one thing, but he didn't have that in mind."

"That's for sure."

I went back inside and borrowed a piece of rope and tied Pete's hands behind his back, and when I'd finished I stood up to see the marshal standing there watching me.

"What are you going to do with him now?" he asked.

"I was figuring to take him on down to jail and let you enjoy his company."

"Going to charge him with anything?"

I thought about it. Pete had friends, plenty of them. If I said he'd threatened to shoot me, he would have had more alibis than he knew what to do with. "No, hell. He's drunk and jail's the best place for him until he gets sober enough to think about it. I guess he can go home when he sobers up."

A smile creased Scott's face. "You're getting smart, Charlie. Not what I'd call brilliant, but smarter than you was."

"Who's minding the store for you?"

"I asked that kid of your brother's to watch them for a while. I'll take Pete down there and let him join the gang."

I watched the marshal walk back down the street, and then I went inside and buckled my gunbelt back on and went to supper. It was colder than scat walking, but Mrs. Durning had a good beef stew, and that made things look a whole lot brighter.

There's something that happens to a man who's just had a reprieve from death. First of all, you're grateful that you're still alive and kicking. But then you get to thinking that somebody else got you out of the jam, and then you don't feel too good about it at all. You had to have help, you had to rely on somebody else, and the thought crosses your mind that someday you won't be able to get out of the jam by yourself and that somebody else isn't going to be around. You feel kind of small and insignificant, and if you're half-way smart, you start getting scared.

I went up to my room and thought about a number of things, about how Whiskey was getting along, about why Tom Scott had chosen Bill's clerk to watch over a couple of fast shootists with at least one murder under their belts, and finally about why poor Sara had killed herself and her unborn child. That last kind of held my attention, because I'd never really thought too much about it. One thing that came to mind was that she'd wanted to punish the father. I mean, who else would be hurt by it? Well, I was, but that was kind of an accident, if you know what I mean.

The one who would really get hit over the head was the father, and the reason she hadn't done it until then was probably because she still had hopes that he'd step out and own up to his paternity and marry her. But once she'd married me, she'd known that that would never happen, that she'd just go on living with a man she didn't love for the rest of her life, perhaps knowing that the father of her child hadn't cared enough about either her or the child to do the right thing.

But the minute she took her own life, she was putting the blame for that squarely on his back, and he'd live the rest of his life knowing that he'd once loved somebody, for however short a time, and that there would never be anybody else who would care for him half so much, and that he'd killed that love. At least that's the way I figured she must have thought.

17

By the time I got done figuring all that out, I brushed my hair and put a little shine on my boots and set out to see Whiskey. I looked in the dining room to see if Tom Scott was eating a late supper, but nobody was there. Mrs. Durning called to me from the kitchen to ask me if I'd seen the marshal. "I'm keeping some stew hot for him," she said. "You tell him to get a move on if he wants any."

"Yes, Ma'am. He's a tad late because he had to run a drunk in, and he's got those two other fellows to keep an eye on."

"Well, you just tell him, Charlie."

"I will," I said, and then I walked out into the cold night and the snow and the wind.

I didn't expect to see anybody out walking, and I didn't. I might have seen Tom Scott coming back from the jail to his late supper, but I didn't even see him. There was a light showing in Bill's store, but I guessed there wouldn't be any customers in there, any more than there would be in Sol Levitan's place. Everybody with any sense and no errands would be huddled around the stove in his own home tonight.

Mrs. Meyer opened the door for me. "She just ate some beef broth," she told me. "I think she's feeling a mite better, Charlie."

"Can I go up?"

"Well, of course. Only, if she's sleeping, don't wake her up, mind."

"I won't."

I hauled myself up the narrow staircase and tried to keep my boots from clumping too loudly on the bare floor, and I went into the room where a little night lamp was burning on a stand near the bed. Whiskey opened her eyes and smiled at me. "I was waiting for you," she said.

"Well, I'm here now."

She gestured toward the music box. "Wind it, please?"

I turned the key with a series of little clicks and put it down near her so she could reach the lever. "Can you get it from there?"

"Sure thing." She stretched out her hand, and I was surprised to feel how thin and cold it was.

I bent over and kissed her, very gently, and then I sat down on the chair beside her and kept holding her hand, as if in some way I could warm it.

She dozed for a while, and then she opened her eyes again and we talked about the kind of house we'd put up out on the Picken place, once we filed a claim. I thought of how comfortable it would be, just the two of us, on a cold night like this.

"I want to sleep now, Charlie," she said finally. "Why don't you go down to Jim's and see if you can stir up a game?"

"I'll stay if you want me."

She smiled. "No. I don't need you to watch me sleep." Her hand reached out and touched the lever of the music box, and then I kissed her again and said goodbye and walked out. The tinkle of "O Promise Me" followed me down the stairs.

* * *

In all probability there would be no game at Jim's Emporium, so I turned in the other direction and went toward the edge of town to Bill's house, mainly out of curiosity.

There was a light in the parlor, coming from a pretty flowered china lamp on a reading table, and I could see Bill and Mary Lou sitting at it, one on each side. I went up the steps, taking care to make noise enough so they'd know they were getting company.

Bill seemed surprised when he opened the door and saw me, but he was friendly enough, for a change. "Come on in, Charlie. Have a cup of coffee with us."

Mary Lou gave me a shy smile and went out to the kitchen to fetch the coffee, and it crossed my mind that she too was getting awful friendly all of a sudden, but I didn't pay it too much attention.

Bill was thirty-four and a good-looking man by anybody's standards. He was wearing black broadcloth, although he'd shed his coat like any sensible person, and his chest still showed good muscle and not too much fat, considering that he was essentially a sedentary person. Well, so was I, for that matter, and fat never troubled me.

"You seem to be quite a hero," he said.

I shrugged, but I wondered at the way he'd put it. No congratulations over a hard job well-done, no friendly I-knew-you-could-do-it boy, like you'd expect from even a half-brother. Instead it seemed to be bugging him that I'd managed to become respectable. I put it down to jealousy: it was probably something he couldn't have even tackled, let alone done.

"What will happen to those two fellows?"

"They'll wait in jail until the circuit judge comes, and then they'll stand trial. I'd guess they'd be put away for maybe five years or so for attempted murder."

"That seems like a long time."

"For murder?"

He shook his head. "I didn't mean that. I'm only thinking that five years might be a good incentive to break out of jail."

"I don't think that's about to happen," Mary Lou put in. "Charlie will simply go get them back if they do."

"That's me. The fellow who goes after them."

Bill smothered a yawn and excused himself. "It's been a long day," he said. "Up at six—well, you know how it goes, Charlie."

"I remember." I finished my coffee quickly and stood up. "You two take care of yourselves. I'm going to mosey around and see what's happening."

Bill saw me to the door. "You take care now," he said, and it struck me for maybe the thousandth time how weak and scared he really was, underneath the mask of the successful businessman.

The lamp was burning in the marshal's office, so I went over there to see what Tom Scott was up to. Or maybe it was just to look through the bars and see Sam Bonner getting a taste of what he was going to put up with for the next several years.

But any complacency I had when I touched the doorknob vanished when I opened the door. The office was empty, one cell-door was open, and somebody was lying with his feet sticking out the door. I drew my revolver, checked the room, and went over to the cell. Scott had been hit over the head, judging from the big lump alongside his ear, and his hands had been tied behind him. There was no sign of Sam Bonner or Dutch Evarts or Pete Moffatt, nor of the clerk Tom had recruited to stand guard.

I cut Tom's binding to free his wrists, and then I hauled him to a sitting position against the wall. He blinked a couple of times, and then he roared like a bull, "Where the hell are they?"

"Seems like you'd know more about that than me."

He shook his head. "Somebody hit me over the head when I come in. I seen the boy setting there at the desk like he was supposed to be, and then next thing I knew, there was somebody behind me laid a pistol barrel alongside my head."

"Where's the kid?" I asked, but I had a feeling I already knew. I went over to the cell with the closed door, and there he was, laid out on the cot, all trussed up with a gag in his mouth.

I got him loose and told him to start talking, and by that time Tom had splashed cold water on his head and come over to hear it.

"They tricked me," he whimpered. "One of them asked me for a drink of water, and when I went over, he put an arm around my neck and pulled me up tight against the bars. I blacked out for a little, and then they were all loose. Must've got the key from my belt. They told me to sit at the desk and wait for the marshal. They had a gun on me all the time, and there wasn't nothing I could do."

"By that time, no," Tom Scott snorted. "Hell, you lost the whole game as soon as you went near that cell."

151

"Can I help?"

"Hell, no," I told him. "Get yourself home and try not to get run over by a stray jackrabbit on the way."

Predictably, Sam and Dutch and Pete had taken their own weapons, except for a missing Winchester. The rest of the guns were in good shape; they hadn't taken the time to disable them.

"All right, where do you want to start?" I asked the marshal.

He poured coffee into two mugs. "Let's not go off half-cocked. We've got three of them to fight, and the thought ain't pleasant. We got to do some figuring."

"That won't take long. Two of them want the money I won off them, one of them wants to kill me by slow degrees, and none of them would cry at my funeral."

"Money," he said. "They'll head for the Emporium and your rooming house."

"It's not there," I grinned. "Dumb I am, stupid I'm not."

"Good," he approved. "All we have to do is try them two places first."

"All right. And we've got to cover the livery stable, because Sam and Dutch are going to make tracks out of here the minute they don't find money in my room, because they've got attempted murder facing them."

"More'n likely, they're going to hang around to get the money," Tom Scott disagreed. "They know there's not apt to be a trial for a couple of weeks."

"All right—do you feel up to going out there?"

"Hell, yes, and we better get moving before they smarten up and come back here."

Tom Scott helped himself to one of the Colts in the desk, loaded it, and checked his gunbelt. "Need a

152

spare?" he asked.

I patted the Starr. "I'll stick with this and one of those Winchester rifles, if you can spare one."

He reached for the rack and took one down. "This one here's a .44-40. I'll give you a box of shells you can use for it. They'll fit your Starr too."

I thanked him and broke open the box and loaded the rifle and filled my belt loops. I stuck the extra rounds in my pocket.

"All right," Tom Scott said. "Let's go. Remember, these men are felony suspects. You can shoot on sight."

"They will too," I told him, and then we walked out into the night.

There was still a lamp burning in the window of Bill's house, but that didn't have to mean much. Maybe he hadn't been as tired as he thought. We walked down the street, checking the spaces between buildings before we crossed them, paying careful attention to windows and doorways. Tom Scott took the south side and I took the north.

When I came to Doc Meyer's house, I held up my hand and pointed. The marshal nodded and I tapped on the door.

The minute I saw Mrs. Meyer's face, I knew the worst.

"I'm awful sorry, Charlie. Doc did what he could, but she's back in a coma, and we don't know if she'll make it or not."

Something in me seemed to harden, the way steel can harden when you quench it in cold water, and I knew I'd passed some kind of stage in my life. I had never felt I could kill a man, that disarming him and putting him in jail would be about the extent of my aggression. Now I knew that wouldn't be enough. There was nothing left to stop me any more.

"Did you want to go up and be with her?" Mrs. Meyer was saying.

"I can't, ma'am. I've got to help the marshal. Those fellows escaped from the jail house, and they're out in the town somewhere looking for me."

She nodded. "I understand. You watch out now, Charlie. We'll take care of her until you get back."

"I thank you kindly," I said. There would be a time for crying or howling or just plain cussing later, but this wasn't it.

18

Mrs. Meyer closed the door and I crossed the street to where the marshal was waiting. "She's in a coma," I told him.

"I'm sorry to hear it, Charlie. You want to back out of this, you can."

I shook my head. "I've got a personal stake in it. There's no way I'm going to let them go."

"All right then." He looked as if he wanted to tell me something, but he only said, "We'll keep on down the street to the Emporium. I'll go in first, and you stay behind me and back me up. Then we'll go on down to Mrs. Durning's and see what we can find out."

Sol Levitan's store was closed now. There were no lights and the door was barred with a two-by-four, the way Sol generally did. We worked our way down the street until I stood at the corner of the Emporium. Tom Scott crossed the street, stood in front of the door for a moment, and then slammed it open against the wall and went in fast, staying to one side. I followed him and closed the door as soon as I saw there was nobody there except for Jim and a couple of town loafers.

"They've been and gone," Jim said. "Three of them are looking for you, Charlie. They helped themselves to a bottle of whiskey apiece and lit out."

"I'm looking for them," I said. "Did you see which

way they went?"

"Nope. They come in here with guns out, and that's the way they left. I wasn't about to follow them."

"All three of them?" the marshal asked.

"Two of them come in, Pete and Sam. Dutch was right outside the door though. I seen him standing there when they first come in. They grabbed off a bottle for him too."

"Let's go," the marshal said to me.

"Charlie?" Jim said. "You think you can handle this?"

"What do you mean?"

"I mean, this is where the cards are down on the table. You better be damn sure you can kill a man before you go after those three. It's not going to be enough to be fast or good. You're going to have to bet your life against theirs."

"Whiskey's dying," I said flatly, and it sounded like somebody else had said it.

"All right, then," Jim said, satisfied, "One other thing, Charlie. But you watch out for that fourth man."

Fourth man? And all of a sudden it clicked. Of course there was a fourth man. The one who'd set Pete against me. The one who'd deserted poor Sara. I had a bitter taste in my mouth. Whiskey had been caught in the middle of something that was none of her doing, and she was paying for it with her life.

"I don't need to name no names, do I?" Jim asked.

I shook my head. "Not any more. I'll handle it when I get to it."

"Come on, Charlie," the marshal said.

* * *

A determined and angry Mrs. Durning was sitting at her kitchen worktable with an old Walker Colt in front of her. "Those danged outlaws came in here without so much as a by-your-leave," she said. "All of them drunk as skunks and cussing and belching. And where were you, Tom Scott?"

The marshal looked sheepish. "I left them locked up, Ma'am. The kid who was supposed to watch them got careless."

"Well, I should say. Now you go catch them and put them where they belong!"

"We're about to do that, Mrs. Durning." He looked dubiously at the old revolver. "You might do more harm than good with that thing, if you don't mind my saying so. These men are expert shots."

"It didn't do much good my sitting here unarmed. I'll try it this way."

He shrugged and we went on up to my room. The bed had been overturned and the breech-block was out of the Sharps. I rummaged in the bedding and located it, together with the extractor and the pin that holds the breech-block in the receiver. They hadn't been smart enough or sober enough to throw those out the window.

"Don't waste time with that," the marshal ordered.

"It'll just take a minute." I got the rifle reassembled and put a round in the chamber. "If we need a backup, we've got it."

We went out the back way, checking the little garden with its picket fence before we left the cover of the house, and then we worked our way down the alley.

Time was important, because if any of the three had sense enough to check the jail, they'd know the marshal was with me and that they had two men to deal

157

with instead of one. But when we got to the jail, the front door was open. They already knew.

"What do you figure?" I asked. "Split up or keep on like we've been doing?"

"Dunno. Might as well split up, I guess. Meet me at the Emporium in about half an hour, and we'll see what we've got. If you hear any shooting, come a-running."

"Sounds good to me."

Somewhere back in the years Stud Walker had told me about how General Longstreet and General Jackson had split forces to hit the Union Army. It had really been General Lee's idea, I guess, but it sounds like the sort of thing that wins battles because it's unexpected. Tom Scott must have had the same idea in mind when he suggested we split forces.

I crossed the street to the south side fast, and came out just east of Bill's new house. The light was still on in the parlor, and I stayed far away from the house so I wouldn't be silhouetted by it. And then I saw three men come out of the shed in back of the house and start heading for town.

I cut in between a couple of buildings and came up to where I could see them when they went by in the street. I figured I'd wait until they passed and then call on them to surrender. One warning shot would bring the marshal, and then back they'd go to jail. I still wasn't ready to shoot on sight, the way the marshal had warned me I might have to do. Not that I wasn't tempted. When Mrs. Meyer had told me Whiskey was dying, I knew that I'd never rest easy until justice was done.

But it takes a while for a lifetime of Thou Shalt Not Kill to get overcome, even with a provocation like mine, and I still had an idea I could get three drunk and crazy shootists to lay down their weapons.

It took me about five minutes to get a funny prickle in the back of my neck, the warning that somebody's working up behind you, and I forced myself to hunker down beside a rainbarrel and listen. Sure enough, somebody must have spotted me going between the buildings, and two of them were in behind me while the third one was out in the street. I saw the two silhouettes against the snow at the south side of the buildings, one on each side, and the only edge I had now was that they didn't know I knew they were there.

I looked over my shoulder, and I couldn't see the third man, but I knew he had to be out there somewhere, probably waiting for me to come running out in the middle of the street where he'd get a clear shot at me. When I turned around again, I saw one of the men slide around the corner and come down the space between the houses, walking slow and careful, like he was treading on eggs. I could see the other man covering him from the corner. I guessed that when the first one got to the rainbarrel, he'd do the covering, and the other one would come in searching.

There wasn't a hell of a lot of time, and if the man out in the street came to the opening, he'd spot me in a minute. They might not shoot to kill immediately, because they'd need to find out where I'd put the money, but being dead now or in half an hour wasn't much of a difference. I lined up the shot with the rifle still down on my knees, and then I stood up fast and levered shots to one side of the passageway and the other. Somebody yelled and I ran toward the two men, or at least to where they'd been. One had been hit, because I saw him limp around the corner. The other was long gone, driven back by my fire.

I got to the corner and looked around it, crouched well down. Tracks in the snow led down to the creek, a natural kind of trench, if you wanted to look at it that way. A slug popped past me, coming from the street, and I scuttled around the corner and raced for the next building over, reaching it just in time, because two wild shots from the creek came thunking into the wood siding.

There wasn't much time for any clear thinking, but I found shells in my pocket and reloaded the rifle as I ran. When I got back to the street, I huddled in a doorfront and waited to see what would develop. Old Tom Scott was standing just in front of Sol Levitan's store, kind of blending in with the outline and keeping an eye on me. I lowered my rifle and came out cautiously, looking right and left. Nothing moved, and I called softly to the marshal. Then I went over and told him what had happened.

"They damn near got you that time," he growled. "You got to watch out for them mistakes."

"What mistakes?" I said heatedly. I thought I'd done pretty well.

"You figured you could see them, but they couldn't see you. That was the big mistake." He spat in the snow. "They was waiting for us to come to them, and when you come around back of that house, they spotted you and damn near had you."

"I guess you're right," I admitted. "How are we going to get them out of the creek bed?"

"We're not," he said. "We're going to let them come to us. If we try to drive them out of there, one or both of us is going to get shot, and I'm in no great hurry to pass to the Great Beyond."

So we waited it out, splitting again, one to the east and one to the west, and watching the ravine. Tom Scott was old and maybe slow, but he had years of experience behind him, and I was young and hot-headed, but I had enough sense to know he was right. The three of them weren't going anyplace in this weather unless they had horses, and probably not even then. They were going to get that money first. Sooner or later, the cold would drive them to get into one of the houses, and that was what we were waiting for.

I was cold as death warmed over, but at least I was in the shelter of a house to keep the wind off my back, and they were looking into the wind, if they were looking at all. Best of all, we knew where they were and they didn't know where we were.

It must have been half an hour later when I saw movement to the east of me, and I knew they'd followed the ravine to get to the other edge of town and head for the livery stable. I waited until the man got in the open, and then I tracked him with the Winchester and fired. He went down in the snow, but then he was up again and running for shelter. I swore. It was the second time I'd missed tonight.

But there was one good thing about it. The other two were probably still down in the creek bed. I'd managed to split them up.

Tom Scott came up behind me. "Are the others down there?" he wanted to know.

"I saw one of them, but I missed him. I guess the other two are still there."

"But you don't know."

"No . . ."

A shot blasted just behind me, and I heard the marshal groan and go down. I saw a shadow pass quickly across the space between the houses, and I got to the street end in time to see it dart across. This time I dropped the rifle and drew the Starr. I took my time with the shots, firing only when I had the sights lined up, and then firing three in quick succession. This time the man went down as if somebody'd pushed him. He didn't get up.

"Get him?" Tom Scott murmured behind me.

"Yes, he's down for good." I turned to him. "Where are you hit?"

"Right shoulder."

"Get across to Doc Meyer. I'll cover you."

He gripped me with his left hand. "No. You look at it and tie it up. I can't move too much, but I can sure as hell do more good out here than I could in Doc's house."

I opened his sheepskin. The front of his shirt was already wet with blood, and when I tore open the shirt, I could see the hole. I wadded up a handkerchief and held it over the wound, and then I told him to hold it in place.

"There's a strap in my coat," he said. "Put it on top and cinch it tight. I can still use the arm, I think, but I don't want to move it too much."

"Sure." I secured the pad with the strap and buttoned his shirt over it again. "I wouldn't try to shoot that rifle."

"Don't worry, I won't. If I was you, I'd get over to the stable and see if you can stop them from getting horses."

I nodded and set out, staying on the south side of the street where I could watch the front door of the stable and the street as well. The man I'd shot was lying where he'd fallen, and the lights had gone out in

162

the Emporium, either because it was late or because Jim was playing cautious.

Nothing moved, which didn't prove much of anything. I took time to reload the three empty chambers in the Starr, and then I went slow and easy down the street. I reached the east end of town and still I could see nothing. About that time I realized that they could move in the ravine in two directions without being seen, and that they had probably gone west, either to get around me and take me from the rear, or to work around the west edge of town. The fact that the marshal had been shot from the street end of the building proved that they were behind me, and I swore at my slowness in catching on so late. The one consolation was that Marshal Scott was somewhere behind me, covering my rear.

I took a chance and sprinted across the end of the street, peering through the gloom to see if anyone was coming at me, but nothing moved and I reached the Emporium and called softly to Jim.

There was no answer, of course. Jim had closed the doors and bolted them, like a prudent man, and he and Martha were probably in back or upstairs in their room. I debated whether to bother them and decided not to: the stable was the answer. If I could keep them on foot, they'd be a lot easier to handle.

I slipped around the side of the Emporium and worked my way to the alley. There was enough light from the stars to see where I was going, but every shadow was a potential hiding place.

Looking at the situation the way a gambler will, I decided that the odds had changed against me. First it had been three against two; now it was two against one. I couldn't count on Tom Scott; if the shot that hit him had broken his shoulder, he'd be out of the fight. But I wasn't going to sit in the alley and worry about it. The only way I could beat the odds was to hunt Sam and his friend down before they could get to me. That way I'd have the advantage of surprise and of picking my own ground. It was about the only advantage I'd have.

There was a lantern burning in the stable; I could see the yellow light through the cracks between the planking. Joe Huntly was probably in there sleeping; although he was pretty fanatical about nobody smoking in his stable, he insisted on sleeping with a light. I got up close to a crack and looked inside. I saw pretty much what I expected to see, which was nothing, and I moved to go to the east side and find another crack from which I could probably see more.

And froze. I'm not the smartest person in the world, but I can recognize a gun when the muzzle is jammed against my neck.

If I'd have thought quicker, I probably could have ducked, turned, and swung a punch, but I didn't. I froze, and Sam Bonner chuckled and said, "That's right, sonny. Just go to the door nice and easy and open it. We got business to take care of."

It was warmer inside, but not by much. The wind came through the cracks, and every so often the lantern flickered in a draft. Sam shoved me forward after he'd relieved me of my guns, and I fell into a bale of hay, which was lucky for me, because Joe hadn't cleaned out the passageway for some time.

In one of the stalls I saw the pale face of Joe Huntly peering out at us, as if the world had started moving too fast for him to comprehend, which it generally did.

"All right, Charlie," Sam said. "I got a good deal for you. You give me my money, and I'll let you live. All you got to do is tell me where you put it, and then you walk out of here, free as the air."

"You're forgetting something, Sam. You shot a girl."

He shrugged. "There's other girls, Charlie, but you only got one life. You want to think about that real hard."

I pretended to think about it, and then I grinned at him. "Tell you what, Sam. Maybe we can strike a quick dicker here."

"I told you already what the choice is. Don't make me have to work it out of you the hard way."

"I just want to sweeten the pot a little. I'll tell you where the money is, if you tell me who told you to come to town in the first place."

He laughed. "You're a real card, Charlie. A regular joker. Why, nobody told me to come here."

I shook my head. "You're lying, Sam. Somebody set you on my trail, and I want to know for sure who it was and why."

Like I've said, Sam was a big man, but that didn't mean he couldn't move fast when he wanted to. He laid the barrel of his Colt alongside my head, right where the slug had creased me when they shot Whiskey and me, and I went down into blackness.

When I came to, I was bound and cold and wet. Sam was putting down a bucket of water with which he'd drenched me, probably to bring me around so I could talk. I shivered and sputtered, and then the scene came clear again. I thought about the useless revolver in my boot, the hideaway gun I'd picked up from Red James's body. It wasn't going to do me much

165

good at all, the way it looked.

"Let's get down to business," Sam said. "Where is it?"

There's no sense fooling yourself that you won't talk if you're in enough pain; everybody's got a breaking point.

Sam put his gun away and took out a large clasp knife and held it against my throat. "Where?"

I shook my head. "You can't kill me, Sam. Not until I tell you where it is, and I'm not about to do that." I started thinking, but it was like swimming through molasses. I could tell him a lie and he'd have to check it out to make sure I hadn't tricked him. It would buy me time, but sooner or later he'd be back with Pete or Dutch, whichever one I hadn't killed, and then it would all have to start again.

He ran the knife down my cheek, and I felt the sudden wetness of blood. "Where?"

I saw movement in the shadows behind him, and suddenly Sam went down like a shot pig. Joe Huntly was standing there with a whiskey bottle he was holding by the neck. He looked as surprised as I felt.

"Get his gun, Joe!" I hissed. "Quick!"

Joe could move fast when somebody told him what to do. He grabbed Sam's gun and mine, and then he cut me loose with Sam's clasp knife. I got my arms and legs working again and decided that, outside of a couple of farriers shoeing horses inside my skull, I was fine. I picked up the riata Sam had used to tie me and went over to tie him. My fingers were stiff, and it took me a tad too long to make a knot. While I was fumbling around, Sam kicked my feet out from under me and made a lunge to get up.

This time Joe didn't move fast enough. I didn't

either. Sam made a pass at my gun, missed, and kept on moving. I threw a shot at him as he went through the door, but I could tell I'd missed him clean. A .44-40 at close range is like getting hit in the middle with a two-by-four. The man goes down and stays down. Nothing had touched Sam.

Joe looked terrified. "I guess I should have watched him better, Charlie."

"It's all right, Joe," I told him. "But when he figures out who conked him with that bottle, he's going to be kind of mad. Here, take this." I reached in my boot and got out Red James's gun and handed it to him. "Make yourself scarce around here, unless you figure to help."

"I'm no hero," he said truthfully enough, and he motioned to one of the stalls. "I'll just stay here and keep them from getting to their horses."

"That's helping," I told him, and then I went out into the wind, where the cold made my wet clothes crackle with ice in a minute. I told myself that the cold would also make me a little more alert, and for a time I believed it.

I tried to figure what they would do next. Sam would be smart enough to know that I wouldn't hang around the stable waiting for them. My only hope of surviving was to stay on the move, trying to get a lick at them where they least expected it. They'd have to trap me on the run, and I was sure Sam knew that too.

The closest haven was Mrs. Durning's, and I went to the back door, called out to her, and went in, hoping she had recognized my voice and wouldn't shoot. She had, but she still had her antique cannon of a revolver leveled at me across the table. "What do you want now?" she demanded. "You come to town and all of a sudden it's a place where a decent person can't live in peace."

"Not my fault people want to kill me," I said. "If they come for me, I'd be obliged if you didn't tell them I was here."

"I'll do that much for you," she conceded. "You want something to wrap around your head?"

I stayed long enough to let her tie a piece of sheeting around the wound Sam's blow had reopened, and then I legged it up the stairs and stuck the Winchester under the mattress and hauled out the Sharps. It wasn't fast, but at least I could shoot it better than the lever gun.

The street seemed empty when I checked it from the side windows, so I went out the front door as bold as you please, and then I headed west, toward Doc Meyer's place. If they had any idea Whiskey was still alive, they'd try to trap me there. The one consolation I had was that the marshal was probably still there, letting Doc fix up his arm enough to keep him from bleeding to death. Even wounded, he'd be able to protect Whiskey.

It was a long, slow walk, because I had to check the space between each building and the next, both on my side of the street and the other, before going on. On the way I passed the body of the man I'd shot, but I wasn't curious enough to stop and see who it was. It didn't really matter. He was someone who had wounded the marshal and who would have killed me, if he'd had a little more time.

Mrs. Meyer let me in when I told her who I was, and I found Tom Scott lying on the couch in Doc's office. "He's in no shape to go hunting killers," Doc said in an even voice. "Your lady friend upstairs is in pretty

168

bad shape—worse than the marshal. I think the best thing you can do is get out of here before they find you and kill us all."

"Kind of you, Doc."

"What in hell do you want out of me, Charlie?" he demanded. "You come to town and people get shot and killed or wounded. There are two people here right now who wouldn't be here if it hadn't been for you."

I exploded. "You dumb sonofabitch, if you and the rest of this sanctimonious town had had the guts to face facts five years ago, none of this would have happened. You ought to be thinking about the man who brought these killers in and putting the blame where it belongs."

His eyes widened. "What do you mean, 'guts'? And what's that got to do with five years ago?"

"The whole damned town let me get beaten within an inch of my life for something that was in no way my fault, and nobody did anything to stop it. Your chickens are coming home to roost, Doc, and if my skin weren't at stake, I'd be tempted to ride out and let you clean up the mess yourselves."

He started to say something, but I turned around and walked out. There was nothing he could say that would change anything. As I went out, Tom Scott winked at me. It was about all the approval he could muster, doped up like he was on Doc's tincture of laudanum.

I wasn't thinking too much of Tom Scott right then. I wasn't even thinking about Whiskey lying up there dying. I was thinking about the odds. They were two to one without the marshal even making a half. I was thinking about how I'd tried to keep killing out of Caliope, and for thanks I was getting no help from anybody except Tom Scott and the hostler, Joe Huntly.

Thinking of Joe reminded me that I had to find a place to spend the night. It was past midnight, and there was nobody I knew who I could trust to put me up. Maybe Sol Levitan, but I wasn't going to wake him up in the middle of the night and tell him that all I wanted was a place to sleep out of the wind, and that if anybody came looking for me he might get his place shot up a little bit, but not to mind.

In the long run, there was only one place I could go, the stable, and I went there, ducking behind buildings and scampering across open spaces, skulking in shadows, and scared out of my wits half the time.

The body in the middle of the street was sifted over with blowing snow now, probably frozen stiff. I looked for it as I went behind the buildings, almost as if I needed a reminder that the other two were vulnerable and that, with luck, I might just survive.

I went around the perimeter of the stable, being careful where I put my feet, and watching behind me every so often so I wouldn't be a sitting target for the second time that night. When I got to about where Joe was keeping watch in the stalls, I knocked on the boards and called his name.

There was no sound inside except for the horses stirring restlessly, mine and Whiskey's, the other one of Sam's, and a spare team for the stage, if it ever made it through.

"It's Charlie, Joe," I called softly. "I'm coming in for the night, if it's all right with you."

Still no sound. I told myself he'd had an extra bottle stashed away and that he was drunk and sleeping it off, but it didn't sound right, even to me.

I went around to the big front door and tried it. It swung open a little, and something dragged on the dirt inside. I closed my eyes for a moment, to get them used to the dark, and then I went down on my knees and groped for the thing that was dragging. It was the bar Joe used to secure the doors, and it was in one keeper, on the right-hand door, but not in the other.

I risked a glance inside. The lantern was still burning on its peg, and Joe was lying near the door, arms spread out, like a rag doll that had been flung there. I took the Sharps in my left hand, holding the Starr in my right, and then I went inside.

Somebody had hit Joe from behind, squarely across the neck, probably with a piece of timber. His neck was broken. The gun I'd given him was gone, and so was the riata Sam had tied me with.

I took half an hour to search the barn and make sure the killers weren't hiding somewhere, and then I went in the stall where my horse was stabled, threw down clean straw, and went to sleep. The horse would wake me if anybody came in, but I don't think it would have mattered. I was tired enough to sleep no matter if somebody'd told me fifty Cheyenne warriors were outside waiting to get in.

19

When I awoke, it was light outside, probably around eight o'clock. I'd forgotten to wind my watch, and it had stopped. I found a bucket of water and rinsed my mouth, and then I took a long drink. Nobody was in the stable, and I wondered where Sam and his partner had spent the night. I guessed their guns had bought them a place that was warm and comfortable, and that they were sitting down to a good breakfast. I thought about that good breakfast for a bit, just to get my dander up again, and then I climbed to the hayloft and looked out a crack to see what I could see.

The whole town was laid out before me. I could see the roof of the stage office, next door, and beyond that the top floor of Mrs. Durning's. Most of the main street was visible, and nothing was moving on it except the wind. Sometime during the night somebody had moved the body out of the street; maybe Sam and his partner, although I doubted it. Maybe Purdy, the barber, who doubled as town undertaker.

Way off in the distance, at the other end of town, somebody moved out on Bill's porch and then went back in. I didn't blame them; it was one hell of a cold day. Something else was moving down near Bill's store, and it took me a moment to recognize the clerk, all draped in an old horse-blanket and wielding a broom. I guessed he was getting things in shape before Bill came around to find fault with him. Bill was finicky about the way things looked; he had always put appearance ahead of more important things.

I gave the town a last check, and then I climbed down from the loft and let myself out the back door. Somehow I was going to have to find a way to hunt Sam and his sidekick down and get them separated so I'd have some sort of chance. There was no point in waiting for them to come to me; if they caught up with me in a building, they could simply wait me out until I got hungry or thirsty or desperate enough to come running out, and then they'd take me one way or another. I had no illusions about what Sam would do to me for three thousand dollars. He'd already showed me.

Mrs. Durning was busy frying eggs and potatoes and sidemeat, although I didn't know who she was cooking for, since three of her star boarders were away: Whiskey, the marshal, and me.

"I figured you'd be coming back," she said grimly. "Hungry dogs always come home to eat."

I passed it off and sat down at the kitchen table. "Have any company after I left?"

"None that would interest you. Your no 'count friends haven't come back, if that's what you're asking." She loaded up a plate and handed it to me. "You better eat up and get, before they come looking for you again."

"That's what I aim to do. Still got that horse-pistol handy?"

She nodded toward a shelf next to the stove. "They

173

aren't going to catch me this time. I'll show those bummers a lady can take care of herself."

"Kind of hard-nosed this morning, aren't you?"

She glared at me. "Get anybody else killed last night?"

I pushed my plate away, remembering. "They got Joe Huntly over in the stable. Broke his neck."

"Why'd you have to come back to this town, Charlie? There's been nothing but grief and trouble ever since. Why don't you just get on your horse and get?"

"I did, Mrs. Durning. I didn't notice it made any difference. They just stayed on because the town let them stay. If they'd killed me right off, they still would have hung around to clean out the town. You can't put that blame on me."

"No, I guess not." She motioned to my plate. "Eat up, Charlie, and don't mind me. I get kind of bitter sometimes. I lost my husband that way, you know. Some drunken fool came to town and shot him because he didn't like his looks or some such. I got my reasons."

I didn't say any more. I ate my breakfast and gulped down a hot cup of coffee, and then I put my coat back on and left.

There were a lot of places for hiding, if you had a gun and you didn't mind terrifying people. I didn't know where to begin, so I picked Bill's store. If there was going to be shooting, that was as good a place as any to have it.

It was a lowering morning, kind of gray and brooding. I felt like something was going to happen, but that it wasn't in any hurry to start. The snow was frozen and crusted, but the wind had died down during the night, and it wasn't as cold as it had been. I walked down the street toward Bill's store keeping a careful check on the buildings on either side, but nothing moved, and I got to the store without any more trouble than I'd have had if I'd been going to fetch a new supply of cigars.

I stood off to one side for a moment, checking the street and making my plans. After I had my little talk with Bill, I guessed I'd try to make it to Doc Meyer's and find out how Whiskey and the marshal were doing. Truth be told, I was kind of putting it off. I was afraid of what I'd find.

The clerk was busy dusting shelves, trying to look like he had a lot to do, although it was plain enough that there wouldn't be a lot of business that day, what with the cold and a couple of drunk crazies running loose. My eye caught the polished brass base of a kerosene lamp. It hung low enough so you could see the street outside reflected in it, although it was distorted by the curve. The window of Bill's store made a kind of picture frame, and across the street you could see Sol Levitan's store and even a funny, rubber ball kind of Sol out front sweeping the entrance clear of snow.

"Can I help you?" the clerk asked. He'd apparently recovered from last night.

I continued to watch the street in the lamp. "Half a dozen of those cigars," I told him. "The little thin ones."

I heard him fumble with the box as I reached in my pocket and got out change. For a moment I glanced away at the change, counted it, and put the cigars in my shirt pocket, and then I looked back at the lamp. It was a lot easier looking at the world in distortion

175

than it was looking at it straight, I decided. That had been my trouble. I'd never seen it quite the way it was, only the way I wanted it to be, and that mistake had almost gotten me killed.

"Kind of late for Bill, isn't it?"

"Mr. Pearse sometimes don't show up until nine o'clock," the boy said in an uppity kind of voice.

Something moved in the lamp, something coming to the window and looking in. Something big, with black hair and a black mustache and sharp white teeth under it, and I threw myself back behind a cast iron cream separator as the window exploded from the three shots that spattered into the shelving. The clerk gave a wail and went under his counter, and the Starr bucked in my hands while the next three shots searched for me. One spanged off the cream separator and buried itself in a wall, and two of them found glass bottles along the back wall, and then I was on my feet and at the window.

Dutch Evart was crawling away from the wreckage, one pistol abandoned in the snow, another in his right hand. He got himself away from the wall and propped against one of the posts that held up the porch roof, and then he concentrated on raising the pistol.

"Put it down, Dutch," I told him. "It's over."

But he kept working at it. He grinned at me and pulled away with both hands, but the gun was getting heavier by the minute.

"Drop it."

His face was white and strained with the effort, but he got the muzzle up to where it was pointing at my feet. I saw the blood on his chest, almost where Whiskey had been hit, and then the gun was coming higher and I shot him through the head, cleanly, and he dropped the gun and slid off the post sideways, so half of him was on the porch and the top half in the street. Blood leaked from the back of his head into the snow.

I turned around in time to see the clerk going for his sawed-off, and I let him see the bore of the Starr. "Man just got blowed all to hell out there," I said conversationally. "You want to join him, all you got to do is move."

He froze and I reached over the counter and took the sawed-off away from him, broke it, and stuck the shells in my pocket. I tossed the gun into a space between canned tomatoes and Hofstetter's Bitters, and then I opened the cylinder of the Starr and replaced the empty shells.

Now the odds were one-to-one.

The sun was trying to make up its mind to come through the clouds. It was having a hard time of it. I crossed the street at a run, the Starr in my right hand, the Sharps in my left, and got to the safety of Sol's store. He swung the door open for me and shut it when I was in.

Sol's face was pale, but his eyes were burning and he held his shotgun in one hand, ready for battle. "Who was it, Charlie?"

"Dutch Evarts. I got one last night, must have been Pete. Sam's the only one left."

"Who was it last night?" he asked incredulously.

"Had to be Pete Moffatt. He shot the marshal and then he ran across the street. I got him half-way across."

Sol nodded, like some Old Testament patriarch doing battle for his land and his flocks and his people, and then he said, "I'll help you, Charlie. Just tell me what to do."

He had the right spirit and he had guts, but he didn't have the experience to back it up. I only had last night and this morning to show for experience, but it was enough to do what had to be done. "The best thing for you to do, Sol, is stay here and watch for me. I'm going to go out hunting, and I want to know there's one place in town I can come and hide or get a cup of coffee."

"You've got that, Charlie, any time. You know that."

Sol laid his shotgun down on the counter. "Where are you going to hunt for him?" he asked.

I shrugged. "I don't know. He could be anywhere. I want to go to Doc Meyer's place and see how Whiskey is coming along. And the marshal. He went over there after he got shot last night."

"Was it bad?"

"Shoulder wound's always bad. It was his right one, so he can't use a gun with his good hand. I'm just thinking, if Tom Scott never tried shooting left-handed, he's not going to be able to help himself if that hardcase comes looking for him."

I was thinking about something else too. Where had Dutch and Sam spent the night? Dutch hadn't looked like a man who'd slept out in the cold. They had to have stayed someplace, a safe place where they'd know I wouldn't find them. I tried to consider all the possibilities, but I kept coming back to one place, and that was where I was going to have to go.

New clouds were coming in when I went back outside. They might mean the end of the storm or the beginning of a new one. I wondered if I'd be alive to find out which.

Ordinarily I would have gone west along the street to get to Bill's house, but this was no ordinary day. I cut between two other houses to come out on the south side, and then I made a quick dash for the shed in the rear. I kicked the door open and came in fast, Starr in hand, and felt like something of a fool when I found no one there. There wasn't even as much as a trace of somebody having been there.

I stood well back from the door and examined the rear of the house. Everything looked pretty normal. There was a thread of smoke coming from the chimney in the kitchen, indicating that Mary Lou was busy cooking something. A couple of potted plants sat in the window waiting for the sunshine that probably wasn't coming today.

The next step was the outhouse. All things considered, it was a substantial building, and it was located just about twenty feet from the shed to the west and about the same distance from the house. I went over to it, keeping the door on the side away from me, and trying to watch the house at the same time. Again I found nothing, although I pushed the door open to make sure.

Getting to the house meant crossing twenty feet of what had been the garden two months ago. The potatoes had been dug, the carrots and onions had been pulled, and the earth had been smoothed. I crossed the area quickly and got to a safe spot beside the wall of the house and out of sight of any of the windows. I put my ear to the wall and listened.

At first I couldn't hear anything, but then I picked up Mary Lou humming as she worked and the faint clash and clatter of a pot lid being raised, a metal

179

spoon being put down. All normal sounds, and yet something told me to be careful.

I considered knocking on the back door and going in, and then I decided that another five minutes wouldn't make that much difference. I walked around the house completely, testing each side several times, listening for the sound of breathing or snoring or the creak of a floorboard. When I was satisfied that no one was in the place except for Mary Lou, I knocked on the back door, out of sight of the street, and announced myself.

"Why the back door, Charlie?" she smiled. "Are you selling something?"

"Buying information is more like it."

"That would be man's business, I think. Bill's not here. He went down to the store last night, and I guess he went out early this morning too. I didn't see him, anyhow."

"What was he doing down at the store last night?" I asked, as if it didn't matter a pin to me.

"He said he had to go over the books. He hasn't been too happy with the boy he has working for him." She looked at me strangely. "Why do you ask?"

"Just asking. I was down there a while ago, and he wasn't there."

"He probably stepped out somewhere, Charlie. Now what have you been doing with yourself?"

I accepted a cup of coffee and sat down at the table where I could see the door to the parlor as well as the one to the back yard. "I've been kind of busy staying alive," I told her. "Sam and Dutch and Pete got loose from jail, and they've been trying to corner me. I've been trying to keep it from happening."

"Where's the marshal? Isn't he doing something

about it?"

"He was shot last night."

"Oh, my! And you wanted to see if Bill could help you, is that it?"

I nodded, which is a good way of telling a lie if you have to tell one. "I just wondered if he was around."

"Well, no. Like I said, he went out last night to go over the books. He does that sometimes."

Unwashed dishes were stacked beside the wash pan. I counted four plates and a whole bunch of cutlery, but I didn't let my eyes stay there long. "Pretty little clock," I said, to take Mary Lou's attention off me. "Does the little cuckoo bird come out on the hour?"

"Oh, yes. And it's the cutest thing you ever heard. Bill got it for me a year ago."

I finished my coffee and stood up. "I'd best be going. Maybe I can find Bill down at the store now."

"I'll tell him you stopped by," she said brightly, and she moved between me and the sink, a little too late.

"I'd appreciate that, Mary Lou."

20

It was plain enough that Bill Pearse had had company last night, probably Sam and Dutch. I didn't think Pete Moffatt would have gone there, but you could never tell. At least four people had eaten a meal in that kitchen, and it had been no evening for socializing. It seemed likely that Sam and Dutch had given up the hunt and come back to Bill's house to spend the night out of the cold, and that they had left before I got there. Dutch was out of the way permanently, so that left Sam.

I stopped to figure. If I'd shot Pete Moffatt last night after he shot the marshal, that left Bill and Sam and Dutch to share a meal. The fourth plate would have been Mary Lou's. But that meant Bill was in this a lot deeper than I'd thought. He'd given shelter to two known criminals, criminals, moreover, who were hunting me.

I went a little way along the creek, heading west and out of town, and then I edged my way up the bank and stuck my head up alongside the trunk of a hackberry tree and watched Bill's house for signs of movement.

I waited a long while, using some of my poker-player's patience, and finally I was rewarded by seeing a man go in the rear door. He didn't look like

Bill, and he stayed only a short time before he came back out. He was carrying a rifle, and he headed around the house and toward the street.

Five minutes later I was back on the street, watching him move warily between buildings near Bill's store. I could have picked him off with the Sharps, but I couldn't recognize him, and there was always the chance that he was an innocent third party, as they say in the newspapers. My guess was that it was Sam, but it was only a guess, and once you've shot a man, you can't take back the bullet.

There was a point at which I was tempted to walk down the middle of the street and let whatever was going to happen, happen. But that is about as stupid a move as a man can make. It comes from panic, from fear so intense that it galvanizes a man into action that can only end in his death. If I did that, Sam would snicker, wait for me to go by, and shoot me in the back.

By the time I worked my way down to Bill's store, the man was gone. I hadn't expected him to hang around and wait for me, but I was kind of disappointed anyhow. I was getting almighty tired of waiting to get shot, and I was dangerously close to acting without thinking, just to get the whole thing over with.

The clerk had cleaned up the mess by the time I got there, and he had put a padlock on the front door and gone home, for all I knew or cared. There were some rough boards nailed across the window that Dutch had shot out, and some kind soul had carted Dutch away. I guessed that Purdy was doing a land-office business in corpses.

The next stop had to be the Emporium. If anybody was looking for me, that and Mrs. Durning's would be the places they'd check as a matter of course, and the Emporium was closer to Bill's store. I went between buildings, looking over my shoulder a couple of times to make sure nobody was following me in from the street, and then I went to the back door and knocked softly.

It was good to get into a warm room again, especially one where I didn't have to look over my shoulder to see who was coming up behind me.

Jim and I sat at the poker table in the front room with a bottle and two glasses. "You're safe enough here for now," he said. "But I can't give you no guarantees on how long."

I shrugged. "It doesn't matter much, Jim. I just wanted to get warmed up a little and to find out what's going on."

He smiled. "Seems to me, you're the one knows what's going on, since you started most of it. You shot somebody last night — I don't know where in hell the body went, unless it walked off — and now you say you got another one this morning. That's quite a bit of excitement for a quiet town like Caliope."

"Maybe it's not as quiet as people think."

"How many more get killed before it gets quiet?"

"Sam Bonner, unless he pulls out of the game."

"Do you think he will?"

"No, Jim. Sam's a stand-patter. He won't run. And even if he tried, I don't think I'd let him."

"I figured as much." He poured drinks for us. "You've changed a hell of a lot since you came back here. I guess part of it's growing up, and another part is killing a couple of men. Once that happens, you can't ever go back to the way you were."

I sipped at the fresh drink. "You talk like a man with experience. Did that ever happen to you?"

"It happened," he said flatly. "I never took life cheaply, but after that I never figured I'd hesitate if I had to kill a man. If it was him or me, then it was going to be him."

The wind had started up again outside. It howled around the corners of the building like a tortured devil trying to get in, and the gray light that seeped through the windows did nothing to dispel the gloom.

"Well, I'm about ready to go looking, Jim. I don't think you've got anything to worry about. If he comes in here, tell him I'm waiting on him."

Jim finished his drink and picked up the bottle. "I'll do that little thing," he said, and then he went behind the bar and waited for trade and I went out into the cold wind.

There was one place where Sam Bonner would be safe and warm, much as I hated to think about it, and I headed along the street to check it. Now that Sam was alone, I guessed he'd wait in one place for me to come to him. Maybe he'd be resting, maybe he'd be on edge waiting, but it all added up like the stack of dinner plates on Mary Lou's sink: he'd be at Bill's.

The wind couldn't get through my heavy coat, but it raised hell with my hands, even through the riding gloves I was wearing. I hunched into it and went into the lee of a building where I could watch Bill's house in relative comfort.

For a while there was nothing to see but the smoke coming out of the chimney, whipped almost flat by the wind, but then something moved behind the house, a man going down to the ravine. I watched him until he was out of sight, and then I went to the alley on the north side of the buildings and fought my way in the teeth of the wind to get back to the stable. I wasn't sure Sam would go there, but it seemed like a good place to wait him out.

Joe Huntly's body had been taken away, and there was fresh hay in the troughs and fresh water. Word had gotten around that the hostler wouldn't be working any more, I supposed. I climbed to the hay loft and positioned myself where I could see if anybody was coming to the front door. If they came in the rear, the wind would probably come sweeping through the center aisle and warn me.

There is nothing worse than waiting for something to happen. I got out my watch and wound it, guessing at the time. I tucked my pant legs inside my boots to keep warm. I checked the chamber of the Sharps a half-dozen times to make sure there was a shell in it. Finally I put the Sharps down and took out the Starr and laid it in front of me. And I waited.

The wind died down after a bit, and when I

looked at my watch I saw I'd been there over an hour.

I stayed another half-hour, and then I decided he wasn't coming to the stable after all. He might have decided to go to the Emporium or to Mrs. Durning's and wait for me. If that was the case, I'd have to hunt him down and dig him out, and I didn't like that at all.

21

In the fading light I could see my breath like smoke, and I wondered idly how far away you could see a man's breath. Could somebody outside have seen my breath up in the loft? Well the damage was done now.

I started down the ladder, being as quiet as I could, and I was half-way down when I heard a little noise in the far corner that no horse would make. I was scared and nervous, and the noise did the rest: I missed my footing and fell down the rest of the way. It was the luckiest thing that had happened to me all day, because three shots smacked into the wall behind me, and by that time I was rolling in the dirt to take cover behind the water barrel.

Splinters flew from a post next to me, and I huddled behind my barrel miserable and scared and thinking that if I only trusted Sam Bonner far enough, I'd tell him where the money was and let him ride out. And then I remembered Whiskey, and that turned everything around again. Part of that money had to be Whiskey's, because we'd made plans with it. And Sam couldn't shoot somebody I loved and get away scot-free.

"You coming out of there, Charlie?" he called. There was laughter in his voice; apparently he had recovered himself enough to know where his bread was buttered.

I didn't answer him. For all I knew, he was waiting for me to give away my position so he could come in behind me, although that would be hard to do, since the stalls were at my back and the horses would give him away if he tried crawling through them.

"Tell you what I'm going to do, sonny. I'm going to saddle up and ride out of here, and you can keep your money. How's that sound?"

Like horse apples, I thought, but I didn't answer.

"You're not the kind of fellow to back-shoot a man," he continued. "We're going to do this nice and easy, and nobody's going to get hurt. You already shot my partner, so you got even."

It took me a while to guess what he was doing. He was talking and reloading at the same time, figuring I'd be so busy listening I wouldn't think that he'd fired off four shots out of five, or maybe six, if he kept his cylinder fully loaded.

"You deaf? Or dead?" He paused. "Maybe I ought to come over there and find out."

Boots scuffed in the dirt, coming closer, and when he was maybe ten feet from the barrel, judging from the sound, he stopped. "Last chance, sonny. If I come around there, I'm going to be shooting. I can't take chances with you no more."

I gripped the Starr and waited. The boots scuffed

189

again, but this time he was moving off to the side, perhaps to get a better position. No. He was taking a saddle from its peg. I heard the stirrups drag on the dirt, and then he opened a stall and led a horse out into the walkway. It was a trick to get me to move from my barrel, I guessed. He didn't quite have the nerve to come around that barrel and find out what I'd do about it.

The back door creaked slightly as he opened it, but I didn't move. Somehow Sam had it figured out, and he was watching that barrel as if his life depended on it. Never mind that he'd opened the door, he was still watching the barrel, ready to shoot.

But nothing happened. He led the horse out of the open doorway and mounted.

I listened to the sound of hooves stamping the dirt alongside the stable, and then I stood up, recovered the Sharps from where I'd dropped it when I fell down the ladder, and walked quickly to the other door. I found a crack between boards and peered out. Sam was in the saddle, riding slowly to the west, and as I watched, he disappeared just beyond Mrs. Durning's.

I'd missed my chance, and all because I'd gotten impatient. If I'd waited in the loft, he would have had to come to me sooner or later, and I'd have had an easy shot. I hurried to the back door and slipped out into the night that had come while I'd waited for Sam.

The sky had cleared and the stars were out, so I

could see fairly well. I was careful to stay close to the building and to stay out of the alley. If he was waiting for me, that was where he'd be. I went around the corner of Mrs. Durning's and saw nothing, and then I picked up the sharp-bitten tracks of hoofprints in the snow. They led west, toward Bill's house through the center of town. I followed them warily until they turned off between two buildings, and then I stopped. I could turn the corner and find him waiting for me.

The smart thing to do would be to cut between the two buildings just this side of where Sam had turned off. That way I might catch him in the rear and take him.

There's nothing like being tired and cold to impair your judgment. It beats hot all hollow. I was so busy figuring out how I'd come up behind him, disarm him, and take him to the jail that I clean forgot he had his own plans and that he wasn't stupid. I moved to the corner of the building I planned to skirt, and suddenly the horse was there and Sam was yelling and whooping. He had backtracked and cut his own trail, the oldest trick in the books, and I'd been suckered.

I yelled in sheer fright and jumped backward, and I was almost in time. The big roan chopped my leg with one front hoof and his shoulder caught me and threw me backward as he plunged out into the street. I went sprawling, and Sam reined the horse in and came at me again. I rolled out of the way as the roan whipped past, and then Sam had his pistol out and snapped a shot at me, tearing splinters out of the boardwalk next to my face.

I watched the horse wheel fifty yards beyond, and it was like watching something in slow motion, the horse turning and Sam leveling the revolver, and then I was under a hitching post and backed up against the boardwalk with no place to go. I felt the pain in my leg where I'd been kicked and the blood on my face from where a splinter had caught me, and ducked again as the roan swept past, narrowly missing my left hand and the Sharps.

There was no time for pulling my revolver. I rolled again and sat up as Sam pulled in the roan and began to turn again, and then I thumbed back the hammer on the big Fifty, took a quick sight, and squeezed the trigger.

Sam jerked back in the saddle as if he'd run into a wire stretched across the street, and the horse rushed past like a locomotive with nothing hooked on behind it. Sam slid from the saddle into the street, and the horse dragged him quite a way before he fell loose. His body had torn a furrow, clear through the snow to the dirt of the street, and when I hobbled up to him he was stone dead. The slug had taken him dead center, tearing through his chest and breaking his back.

I sat down in the street beside him and ejected the spent shell from the Sharps and slid a fresh cartridge in, more out of habit than anything else, and I thought about how many men had died for the three thousand dollars they'd hoped to get by killing me and Whiskey. I made up my mind then and there that money was the worst reason for killing a man that there is.

The roan stopped somewhere near the end of the street, and then Sol Levitan came out of his store, shotgun in hand, and walked over to me.

"I came as soon as I could," he said. "It happened so quick, Charlie."

"Yeah. Thanks anyway. If I hadn't dropped him, I sure could have used you."

"Can you walk?"

I shook my head. "I think my leg's busted. I got kicked when he made his first pass."

"Here, I'll help you to the store. Then I'll get the doctor to tend to you."

We made it across the street, me leaning on him and hobbling along in one-legged hops, and when we got inside he sat me down in the high chair at the desk where he kept his books, and I put my head down on my arms on the desk and let it hurt.

22

Doc Meyer came bustling in a short time later, and he and Sol helped me off the chair to the floor.

"How is Whiskey?" I managed to ask.

"Holding her own," he said shortly. "She's still in a coma, but she hasn't got any worse."

"Can I see her?"

He barked a short laugh. "Hell, boy. When I get done with you, you won't be in a mood for visiting."

First off, he wanted to cut my boot off. I objected. "I paid twenty dollars for those boots!"

"A man with your money shouldn't mind. I mean, money was behind the whole thing, wasn't it?"

Sol Levitan cut in quickly. "He had a right to his money, Doc. Now, let me take care of that boot." He had a razor in his hand before he finished speaking, and he cut the stitching so the boot would fall off clean without hurting me, and so it could be restitched.

Doc examined the leg, pulling at it and twisting it slowly, and then he said I had no more than a bad bruise, and that I wouldn't need a cast. "I'm going to rub it with arnica and bandage it, and then you'll have to get you a pair of low shoes until it's healed enough to bear a boot. No riding, no more walking than you have to do. All right?"

I nodded. I was in no position to argue.

Sol came up with a pair of gentleman's shoes that fit just over the ankle. Congress gaiters, they were called. "You just try these, Charlie," he said.

"I only need one," I joked, although the pain was pretty near killing me.

"You can't ride a horse, so you don't need boots," Sol said. "You wear these until you get your leg well. I'll take your boot down to the saddlemaker and have him sew it back like it was. I'll even throw in the crutch for free," Sol said. "You take it and go down to Mrs. Durning's and go to bed for twelve hours. You'll feel like a new man."

"He's right," Doc said. "Stay off that leg for another couple of days, and you'll be fine. You need to heal a bruise as much as you do a broken leg."

"When can I see Whiskey?"

"Maybe tomorrow. That girl needs rest more than she needs you."

Doc went on back to his house and I headed down to Mrs. Durning's.

I made it as far as the Emporium, and then my right arm started to give out, and I turned in without a care in the world except for Whiskey and my leg. I went through the batwing doors, and I managed to get as far as the poker table before I collapsed in a chair.

Jim shook his head ruefully and brought a bottle to the table. "Goddamn if you don't look like a hardcase, if I ever seen one."

"Worse than that, I feel like one."

There were two riders at the bar, both of them bundled in sheepskin coats against the cold. I didn't pay them much mind.

"You keeping count?" Jim asked bluntly.

"Sam, Dutch, probably Pete last night. That's three."

Jim narrowed his mouth. "Them's Pete's riders at the bar."

Pain or no pain, whiskey or no whiskey, I came wide awake. "What are they doing here?"

"Looking for Pete."

"Oh, hell."

He nodded. "Mind your p's and q's and get the hell out of here the first chance you get. You can use the back way."

"Thanks, but I'll stick around. I couldn't run if I wanted to."

In a sense it was a classic situation. The good employees coming to the aid of the boss, just in case he ran into more than he could handle. The villain, who might or might not have killed the boss. The innocent bystander—Jim—who couldn't testify to this or that. The kerosene lamps, impartial, illuminating the whole scene. The unprejudiced green baize cloth on the table, monitoring the action.

"Jim? Get me a pitcher of coffee from the

back, huh?"

Without a word he went away. I had the feeling he was glad to go.

The riders looked at me and I looked at them. It was a case of show or tell, and I wasn't about to tell without some more proof positive, like they used to say in the Deadwood Dick stories.

I wore the Starr on a sliding holster. When I was standing, it rode high on my right hip. When I was sitting at a card table, it rode in a semi-cross-draw position. When you're walking or standing, you want the gun so it meets your hand in a normal draw position: your hand slaps back, hits the butt, pulls the gun, levels and fires almost in one operation.

But when you're sitting, the barrel would catch on your right thigh and slow the draw. Therefore, you've got to position the gun so the barrel is against your left hip and you can slide it out easily and fast and change barrel direction by flicking it in a forty-five degree angle.

Jim came out with the coffee, put it on the table, and went behind the bar. I had a notion he wanted to stay close to his persuader and also out of the line of fire, just in case.

The two riders sipped at their drinks. They were in no hurry. I was sure they'd noticed the crutch and figured out that I wasn't going to be going anywhere in a hurry. They had all the time in the world, and they weren't going to cut it short by rushing. They had their whiskey to drink and their grudge to nurse, and for some folks nursing a

197

grudge is more satisfying than settling it.

I sipped my coffee and played with a deck of cards, just to keep doing something and to keep my eyes off the two. If there was going to be trouble, I wasn't going to be the one to start it.

It took them three drinks to get primed up for what was coming, and then the short one stayed at the bar where he could keep an eye on Jim Hagen, and the tall one came over to the table. He was about thirty, and he had a kind of straw-colored mustache that drooped at the ends. His clothes were worn and faded, but he carried himself like a man with authority, and I guess he was Pete's foreman.

"Your name Pearse?"

I nodded and fanned the cards and folded them back together. "That's what they call me. And yours?"

"That don't matter. I want to talk to you about Pete Moffat."

I shrugged and looked him in the eye. I could see his hands well enough from where I was, and I wanted to keep him from looking at mine. "Go ahead."

"I want to know where he is. He come to town yesterday and he ain't showed back. You know anything about that?"

"Maybe. Somebody took a shot at the marshal last night, and it might have been Pete. Pete got drunk and the marshal locked him up with a couple of hardcases from out of town. They all got loose and came looking for me. Pete might have been the one who shot the marshal."

His eyes were flat, cold. The eyes of a gun-fighter, if I'd ever seen one. "I heard there was more to the story than that. I heard you was the one shot that man in the back."

"You heard right. I dropped him in the street, and then I helped the marshal down to Doc Meyer to get his shoulder tended to. I don't know who the man was. There were two other fellows gun-ning for me, and I wasn't about to take the time to look."

I put down the deck of cards and reached for my coffee. He watched my hand for a moment, and then he looked back at my face. I sipped coffee and put the cup down and dropped my hand below the table. I pointed the index finger of my left hand at him, to give him something to see, and I said, "So you came here to kill me, is that it?"

"If it was Pete you killed," he said. "You've about got the size of it." He let his right hand stray to his belt.

"I've got you covered under the table, friend. I wouldn't touch that gun, if I were you. I'd just back off and walk out of here easy. If it'll make you feel any better, I don't know who I shot out there, but I don't particularly give a damn. He was out to kill the marshal or me, and he wasn't fast enough or good enough to do the job. If it was Pete, he should've known better than to line up with a couple of shootists."

"I think you're running a bluff, Pearse." The

hand quivered.

"There's one way to find out, ain't that right?" I goaded him. "All you got to do is touch that gun, and you'll know for certain."

He made his move and he got his fingers on the butt before I put the Starr up where he could see it. "Pull it slow," I told him. "Use two fingers, and then drop it on the floor."

The man at the bar turned to face me then. I saw him from the corner of my eye as the tall man dropped his gun to the floor, and he sized up the situation and decided not to draw against an exposed weapon. That is a smart decision any time, and it was even smarter that day. I had reached the stage of fatigue and revulsion in which one more man to be killed meant no more than one more whiskey bottle to be shot off a board fence. I got the two men together, just in case somebody had a hideaway gun, and Jim Hagen picked up their weapons and put them behind the bar for safekeeping.

The short one had the most sense and maybe the most guts too. He glared at me and said, "Where in hell did you put Pete's body, Pearse?"

If I'd been him, I'd have shot me for that, but I wasn't. "I've got no idea where it is. Somebody took it off the street after a while. It wasn't too safe to hang around the street here last night and today, in case you didn't know."

"You shot up the town, I hear. Pete was just one of them you shot. That right?"

It seemed to me that he was taking a sentimental approach to the problem. Not too many cow-boys felt that kind of allegiance to the boss. On the other hand, it could have been that he was just looking for a fight to happen, and that this was a convenient excuse.

"You've got no fight with me," I told him. "I shot a man who had just shot the marshal and who was ready to shoot me. The fact that he was running across the street means precisely nothing to me. He made his play, he changed his mind, and he tried to back away from his medicine. That cuts no ice with me."

"Pete never run from nothing in his life," the tall man said. "You're a damn liar."

"How'd I back-shoot him if he was facing his medicine?" I asked.

And then the front door crashed open and I heard a familiar voice. "Floyd, Roy—back off. I got a word with this man."

He was standing there, shotgun in hand, as big as life. Pete Moffatt, none the worse for wear.

23

I watched the barrels of the shotgun start to rise, and I said as quietly as I could, "Drop it, Pete. I can hit you three times before you can pull the triggers."

That was when Jim Hagen saved me a second time. He had his persuader out and leveled, and he said, "If he don't, Pete, I sure as hell will."

Moffatt looked as if he was about to cry. Not because he was in danger of getting his head blown off by a shotgun at the same time I was about to perforate him from the front, but because he wasn't going to be able to kill me. He'd have died happily enough, if he'd been able to accomplish that.

Another gun hit the floor. Jim came around the bar and scooped it up and stuck it in his cubbyhole with the others. "Ought to go in the firearms business," he said to no one in particular.

Pete Moffatt looked his hate at me. "There'll be another day," he said. "You'll never turn around without wondering are you going to see me standing behind you."

"Sit down, Pete," I told him. "I'm going to explain something to you."

"I don't sit with killers."

Jim Hagen grabbed a bottle and a couple of glasses. "Pete, I'd advise you to listen to the man. There's been enough killing in this town, enough hatred. Now we can settle this real easy, if you listen."

"He killed Sara," Pete snarled. "I ain't about to forget that, Jim. I ain't going to forget you throwed down on me when my back was turned, either."

Jim motioned to the two riders. "You boys want another drink, it's on the house. You can get your guns back in the morning."

The two went across to the bar, and Jim set the bottle in front of Pete, almost squarely in the middle of the table. I reached out with my left hand and poured him a drink, then one for me. "Now you don't have to drink with me, Pete. But when I'm done talking, I figure you're going to realize you've got no fight with me and we're going to shake hands and call it quits."

"And pigs'll fly," he scoffed.

I grinned at him, as much to throw him off balance as anything. "I think Jim here knows something I didn't. I think he's always known it, but there was a time he was a little scared to say anything. He let something slip yesterday when I saw him. I figured I had three of you to worry about—you and Sam Bonner and Dutch Evarts. Jim said, 'Watch out for the fourth man,' and I didn't pay him too much mind. Now think about it. If you're sitting here and I killed three men, one of them had to be the fourth man."

Slowly he grasped hold of the idea. "Who'd you kill?"

"I blew Dutch's head off when he tried to kill me over in my brother's store. That's one. I shot Sam out of the saddle when he tried to ride me down two hours ago. The man out in the street last night, he was the fourth man."

"Who in hell wanted you dead that bad except me?" Pete said. "I was always the one to watch out for. And what's a fourth man got to do with killing Sara?"

The two riders at the bar were listening as intently as anyone except Jim. He was safely behind them, his persuader still next to his right hand, just in case.

"He was the man got her in trouble. I'd guess he sweet-talked her a hell of a lot to get her to marry me. He promised her he'd take her and the baby, once it was born, and they'd make some kind of new life somewhere else, and she believed him. Only he wasn't about to give up everything he'd made here, and he sure as hell wasn't about to own up to what he'd done."

Jim looked at me. "You're doing fine so far, Charlie. You might as well figure it out the rest of the way."

"This was a man who knew three shootists were after me. I was fool enough to tell him that and to tell him I'd come up from Wallace. He saw to it word got around Robidoux's store that I was in Caliope with plenty of money, and sure enough they took the bait and showed."

Almost as if he didn't know what he was doing, Pete reached out for his glass and took a sip.

"Now that man tried the worst way to get me out of town, because he figured sooner or later I'd stumble onto his little secret and spoil his plans. He took a shot at me with a scattergun, and it was probably only to scare me. If he'd wanted to kill me then, he would have and could have. But he wanted somebody else to do it for him." I sipped from my own glass, still using my left hand. "That was where you came in, Pete. You were looking for a scapegoat, and he made sure you kept your hate for the man who did your daughter wrong focused on me. When the shootists came to town, he sicced them onto where I was holed up. They shot Whiskey and they shot me, but they didn't kill either one of us. When I came back and trailed them and brought two of them back, something else had to be done."

Jim spoke up from behind the bar. I noticed that his hand didn't get very far from the shotgun. "Ever figure out, Pete, how easy it was for you and them two killers to get out of jail?"

"They knocked out the kid was minding the store for Tom Scott and took his keys."

"Sure," I said. "How'd he get that careless? He could've left the keys on the desk, like he should have done, to bring you all water."

"Never thought of that," Pete admitted.

"But things started to go wrong. I didn't grab a horse and run, the way I had the first time. Well, in a way I was. I hadn't ever killed a man, and I was scared of doing that as much as I was scared of getting killed. But that didn't matter after a while. I was mad enough to go ahead and do it, if it needed being done.

"About that time, he saw I wasn't going to run, so he had no choice but to get rid of me for keeps. I'd guess you were kind of under the weather from whiskey and the hit on the head you got last night, and you went off somewhere to sleep it off. But the other two were still looking for me, and the fourth man went to join them. It was his hard luck that he found me and the marshal together. He probably only saw Tom Scott and shot him, maybe thinking it was me. And then I came up and he ran for it. I got him in the middle of the street with three slugs, thinking all along it was you."

"It makes some kind of sense," Pete admitted grudgingly. "But what about my girl Sara? What happened?"

"This won't be easy to take, Pete, but I've got something a lot harder to swallow, and I'd guess you're man enough to take what you have to." I pushed the bottle toward him. "When I married Sara, I figured I'd make the best of a bad bargain, and so would she. I mean, what the hell, we were both young, and we could make a pretty good life together. A baby's a baby, no matter who its pappy is, and we could have had our own kids later. But what I didn't know was, the father was right there all the time, keeping her quiet by telling her he was going to wind up his business and take her way off to Denver or some such place where they could start life as rich folks. Only I'd guess she kept after him for when he was going to do all this, and he may have gotten mad and called it off.

"I wouldn't say he was worth killing herself over, but she couldn't see far enough ahead that she and I and her baby would have made it fine. All she could see was, she loved this man and he was no good and she'd fix him good. The worst kind of punishment you can give a person is to hang your death around his neck like a millstone. There's very few men can shrug that off."

Pete finished his drink and pushed the bottle away. "Tell me," he said throatily. "Tell me who the bastard was."

The night was wearing old and thin. Smoke from the riders' cigarettes drifted up toward the tin ceiling, and the faint light coming through the front windows made a mockery of dawn. A lot of things were dying that night, loyalties among them.

"For Christ's sake, give him a name," Pete growled.

Jim was watching me across the bar. "Tell him, Charlie," he said. "Tell him who it was."

"The man I killed in the street last night was my half-brother. Bill Pearse."

One of the riders swore. Pete Moffatt looked at me, slack-jawed. "My God," he said. "You killed your own brother."

"I couldn't tell you, Charlie," Jim muttered.

I stood up, holstered the Starr, and gathered my crutch. "Are we quits, Pete?"

He nodded and stuck out his hand. I took it, and then Pete and his riders walked out into the gray light that passed for dawn.

24

Jim watched me for a long moment. I poured a drink, keeping one hand on the bottle, one hand on the glass. He put the shotgun back under the bar.

"Come on over and have a drink with me, Jim. It's been a long night."

"Longer than most," he agreed. "You handled that fine. You got him off your back for good."

I nodded. "It took a little doing, but I guess I did it."

He nodded and poured himself a drink. His hand was steady, a gunfighter's hand. I wondered which sleeve he kept the derringer in.

" 'Course I'm not holding any grudges," I said. "Pete made a mistake and so did I, and there was never much love lost between us. Now, suppose you tell me the truth about Sara?"

"I guess you know by now," he muttered. "I probably was having a hard time with Martha about then, and Sara was handy. She pestered me and I couldn't resist the temptation. That was about the size of it."

"Damn, Jim, you fooled me for a long time. You made me a good offer on the table, you showed me you were my friend, and you even stood up for me against Pete. Twice, once tonight and once last night. You didn't have to do that."

Jim pushed his drink to one side. "Here's how it was," he said. "There was never any question about my leaving Martha, and I told her that flat out at the start, but she wouldn't listen to me. I offered her money to go and have the child, but she wouldn't take it. When you got blamed for it, I wronged you too. I didn't speak up."

"Does Martha know?"

He shook his head. "It would have killed her. And there was never anybody before or anybody after."

"Where did Bill come in on all this?"

His face creased. "He found out, God knows how. He came around to me and told me he had a letter from Sara telling all about us, and he said he'd show the letter to Martha and to Pete unless I wanted to buy it from him. I paid him a thousand dollars for that letter, and I'd bet you money that there's other men in town have done the same. He was a blackmailing son of a bitch, Charlie, and that's the truth of the matter."

I remembered something. "All the time I was talking to Pete, you had your sawed-off on the bar. Who was it for, Jim?"

"Pete," he said quickly. "You know his temper better than most. It sure as hell wasn't for you."

"All right, I'll buy that. So you paid Bill and got the letter. When I came riding in, you made me a good proposition to keep me on your side. Was that it?"

"I owed you plenty, because you took the blame for what I did. It was my way of making it up to you a little bit." He reached for his drink again. "Naturally I wanted you as a friend too, but that wasn't the whole of it."

I watched the early morning creep through the windows as if it was afraid to come in.

"It's over, Jim. As far as I'm concerned, there's nothing between us. You made up for what you did, the best way you knew how, and you saved my life at least once. Let's leave it that way."

He nodded and reached out his hand. I didn't hesitate to take it.

I stopped outside the door and breathed the clean air. My watch told me it was six-thirty, and I decided to skip the luxury of sleeping and go see Doc Meyer. It was early, but I'd been up all night, and I guessed he could bend a rule and let me in.

Mrs. Meyer let me in. "She's about the same, Charlie. She won't know you, but you go on up and sit with her, if it'll make you feel better. You want to go back to the kitchen and wash first?"

"I thank you kindly. I didn't get to bed last night. How's Tom Scott?"

"He'll be all right, Doc says. He went back down to the office."

"I'll drop by there later. Right now I want to see Whiskey."

After I washed I stumped up the stairs and took a chair next to Whiskey's bed. Her face was drawn, but she looked kind of peaceful lying there, as if she knew something nobody else knew and was happy with the knowing of it. I smoothed her hair and talked to her about how it was going to be when we got the claim staked out and a new house built, but I could see it wasn't getting through to her, and after a while I stopped.

The dawn passed that way. Once or twice I went outside to relieve myself, but I came back and finally it was the start of a nice day. I could tell it was warming up some, and I guessed it would be a little while longer before winter set in. The things I could see through the window got sharper, better defined, and almost before I knew it, there was daylight.

Whiskey opened her eyes about then and saw me. She gave me a smile and I bent over and kissed her. "You're going to make it, honey. It's all over, all the fighting."

She nodded encouragement. "I'll try," she whispered. "Honest, Charlie, I'll try."

"It's all over," I said again. "Nobody to bother us any more."

"Sam?"

"He's gone. Him and the others."

She smiled and then she whispered, "I want to sleep now, Charlie."

I sat there a little while longer, and then I went

downstairs and knocked on Doc's door and told him she had regained consciousness.

"That's a good sign," he said. "If she wants to hard enough, she can pull through."

"I'm not much of one for praying, but I did a little of that."

"Can't hurt. Come see her when you can. She'll appreciate that. You'll see her getting better by the hour."

I nodded. "Guess I better get on down and see how the marshal is making out."

Tom Scott looked a lot better than he had the night before. He had some color in his face, and I noticed he'd dug up a left-hand holster from someplace.

"How's your girl, Charlie?"

"She talked to me for the first time. I think she's going to make it. Doc thinks so too."

"Glad to hear that," he said, and then he reached for the drawer that held the office bottle. "What are you going to do now?"

"Play poker, I guess. Wait until Whiskey gets better, and then we'll see about getting hitched and finding a place to live."

"I guess you found out who the fourth man was."

"I found out. Can't say it was too much of a surprise to me, Tom." I guessed he'd meant Bill, and I was right.

"I took orders from him for a long time. When you were in that trouble before, he came by and

213

told me you were to blame and that you ought to take your medicine. I should have looked into it further, but I took his word for it."

I shrugged. "It's water under the bridge now, Tom. I suppose he had something he was holding over your head."

His eyebrows lifted. "As a matter of fact, he did. It was something—"

I cut him off. "I don't want to hear it. That's your business. If it makes you feel any better, I think he was blackmailing a few other folks too."

"I wouldn't be a damn bit surprised," he said. "Hate to say it about your kin, Charlie, but the best thing you ever did for this town was to get rid of him."

I couldn't argue with that.

There were a lot of funerals to take care of. I went to Bill's, although it was against my better judgment. Mary Lou called me a murderer to my face, and her father, the preacher, had some more uncomplimentary things to say about me, but that was about the only opposition I had in Caliope. People I'd never talked to before went out of their way to say howdydo. Folks who'd jeered when I got whipped came up to apologize. Caliope wallowed in its newfound virtue.

And I visited Whiskey twice a day. She was able to sit up in bed after a week. I guess the combination of Doc's skill and his wife's administration of good hot broth were doing the job. Sometimes we talked about the old claim and the new house we'd build there, but mostly we just sat and held hands like a couple of love-sick kids.

I stopped by Sol's place and asked him to make me up a good suit of clothes. "I want a nice suit, maybe black like a gambling man ought to wear. Good worsted material."

"You telling the dog how to bark, Charlie?" he smiled. "For you, my friend, only the best."

"If there's anything I can do for you, Sol, name it. You stood by me when nobody else did. I'll never forget you with that shotgun waiting to see if I needed you."

"A friend doesn't take favors for doing what a friend has to do."

We left it at that. He was right, of course, and I felt just a tad ashamed that I'd mentioned it.

After Sol measured me, I hobbled on down to the Emporium and took my place at the table where I made my living. Jim's wife came out with a couple of cups of coffee, one for Jim and one for me, and we sat down and waited for business. It was early in the day, both for drinking and for playing poker.

"You going to start improving that claim, Charlie?" Jim asked.

I sipped reflectively at the coffee. "I think I'll wait until Whiskey gets well enough for us to get married and move on out there. She ought to have a say in whatever we do."

215

"I guess." He got out a pair of thin stogies and passed me one. "There's winter coming on fast, even if the snow's all but melted. Not much a man can do out on a claim until spring thaw. You ought to buy that land now, though, before somebody else gets on it."

"I've been thinking about that. I'd hate to see some honyocker come along and tear up all that good grass just to plant wheat or corn or some other damn thing that won't survive a Kansas summer. This is cattle country, Jim."

"I agree with you there. So you're going to wait until spring to get started?"

"Seems like the best idea. I talked to Whiskey about it some, and she agrees. We'll probably live up at Mrs. Durning's until the weather's warm enough to move on up there. While she's still recovering, it's best we stay in town. I'll just keep on here, if it's all right with you."

He nodded at me through a bluish haze of cigar smoke. "It's fine with me, Charlie. I got to say one thing though. I'm glad you're getting out of the gambling business. It ain't no kind of life for a married man, and there's not much future in it for a single one either, truth be told."

"Oh, I hadn't planned to make it my life career, Jim. It's a good way to pass the time and make a living at the same time. Besides, it is kind of like life, if you look at it my way. Let me play poker with a man for an hour, and I can tell you what kind of man he is. Brave or yellow. Smart

216

or plumb foolish. Greedy or generous. It all comes out in the cards and the way you play them."

The door opened and I looked up expecting somebody to play cut-the-deck or some such, but it was only Tom Scott.

Jim called back for another cup of coffee, and his wife came out with a mug and the pot. "You fellows going to sit here and drink coffee all day, you might as well have the pot. I can make another one."

He grinned sheepishly. "Well, Martha, there ain't a lot of business right now. Nothing much else to do."

"I ain't complaining, just commenting," she said. "Charlie here don't have much business coming in either. How about you, Marshal?"

"Nothing I can start on this early," Tom Scott said. "Or nothing I want to. I'm a man short, and I don't hanker on working that hard this early in the morning."

When Martha went back to the kitchen, he turned to me. "I might have said this before, Charlie, but I'm going to say it again. I need some help, and you're the best man for the job. You could kind of keep playing poker here and come out when I needed you."

I thought about it, but not too seriously. "Tom, I ain't too much good with one leg bunged up poking along on crutches. I couldn't run or sit a horse. You want to look at it this way, I'm about half a man right now."

"And, I ain't much good with my right arm in a sling. But between the two of us, my legs and your arms, we'd ought to make one pretty good man."

Jim laughed. "He's got you there, Charlie. It'd be a good way of marking time and doing some good to the town while you wait for Whiskey to get well."

I gave it some serious thought while the smoke eddied up from Tom Scott's pipe and Jim's cigar.

On the one hand, I'd killed a total of three men, and it was a thing that didn't come naturally to me. On the other, there wasn't a man of the four who had given me any choice in the matter. No good man had died.

It was a respectable job, and it was one I could handle. Best of all, I'd be helping out the marshal in a time when he needed somebody to help him. I didn't want to see a good man lose his job because he couldn't find a deputy.

"You got this town right where you want it, Charlie," Jim said. "They respect you and they've accepted you as a man who ain't scared to keep law and order. Think on that."

I nodded. "All right, Tom. I'll help you out over the winter until I can get out to the claim and start work. Fair enough?"

"That's jake with me. I can pay you twenty dollars a month just for being around when I need you. In your spare time you can keep on dealing cards."

He grinned like a man who's just drawn his third ace, and he reached in his pocket. "Here," he said, and he pulled out a tin star. "I figured you was smart enough to see reason when you had time to think on it. Raise your right hand and repeat after me."

I raised my right hand and said the words, and for the first time in my life I was a lawman. Truth to tell, it felt pretty good.

After a bit I got up and walked out with the marshal. He was on his way to the office, and I wanted to go back and see Whiskey.

"I'll be back in about an hour, Jim."

"Whenever, Charlie."

The snow was melting in the early morning sun, and there were little pools of water on the boardwalk where the storekeepers had swept away the snow the day before. You could smell the damp wood and the wet earth alongside and the woodsmoke coming from the chimneys of the town.

Tom Scott gave me a printed list of the city ordinances to study, and then I went on down the street to the doctor's house.

Whiskey was sitting up eating oatmeal and taking tiny sips of weak coffee. Doc's wife wasn't up to Jim's when it came to making coffee.

"How's it going this morning, honey?"

"Mighty fine, Charlie. What's that in your hand?"

"I just told a man I'd help him out, and he gave me something to make it official. I figured I wanted you to put it on me and make it special."

She looked at the tin badge and started to laugh. "You a lawman, Charlie? Will wonders never cease!"

But she pinned it on my vest and gave me a kiss to boot. "But only until spring, Charlie."

"Only until spring," I said, and I never in my life meant anything more.

POWELL'S ARMY
BY TERENCE DUNCAN

#1: UNCHAINED LIGHTNING   (1994, $2.50)

Thundering out of the past, a trio of deadly enforcers dispenses its own brand of frontier justice throughout the untamed American West! Two men and one woman, they are the U.S. Army's most lethal secret weapon—they are POWELL'S ARMY!

#2: APACHE RAIDERS   (2073, $2.50)

The disappearance of seventeen Apache maidens brings tribal unrest to the violent breaking point. To prevent an explosion of bloodshed, Powell's Army races through a nightmare world south of the border—and into the deadly clutches of a vicious band of Mexican flesh merchants!

#3: MUSTANG WARRIORS   (2171, $2.50)

Someone is selling cavalry guns and horses to the Comanche—and that spells trouble for the bluecoats' campaign against Chief Quanah Parker's bloodthirsty Kwahadi warriors. But Powell's Army are no strangers to trouble. When the showdown comes, they'll be ready—and someone is going to die!

#4: ROBBERS ROOST   (2285, $2.50)

After hijacking an army payroll wagon and killing the troopers riding guard, Three-Fingered Jack and his gang high-tail it into Virginia City to spend their ill-gotten gains. But Powell's Army plans to apprehend the murderous hardcases before the local vigilantes do—to make sure that Jack and his slimy band stretch hemp the legal way!

**WESTERN STORYTELLER
ROBERT KAMMEN
ALWAYS DEALS ACES WITH HIS TALES
OF AMERICA'S ROUGH-AND-READY FRONTIER!**

MYSTERIES TO KEEP YOU GUESSING
by John Dickson Carr

CASTLE SKULL (1974, $3.50)

The hand may be quicker than the eye, but ghost stories didn't hoodwink Henri Bencolin. A very real murderer was afoot in Castle Skull—a murderer who must be found before he strikes again.

IT WALKS BY NIGHT (1931, $3.50)

The police burst in and found the Duc's severed head staring at them from the center of the room. Both the doors had been guarded, yet the murderer had gone in and out *without having been seen*!

THE EIGHT OF SWORDS (1881, $3.50)

The evidence showed that while waiting to kill Mr. Depping, the murderer had calmly eaten his victim's dinner. But before famed crime-solver Dr. Gideon Fell could serve up the killer to Scotland Yard, there would be another course of murder.

THE MAN WHO COULD NOT SHUDDER (1703, $3.50)

Three guests at Martin Clarke's weekend party swore they saw the pistol lifted from the wall, levelled, and shot. *Yet no hand held it*. It couldn't have happened—but there was a dead body on the floor to prove that it had.

THE PROBLEM OF THE WIRE CAGE (1702, $3.50)

There was only one set of footsteps in the soft clay surface—and those footsteps belonged to the victim. It seemed impossible to prove that anyone had killed Frank Dorrance.

THRILLERS BY WILLIAM W. JOHNSTONE

THE DEVIL'S CAT (2091, $3.95)

The town was alive with all kinds of cats. Black, white, fat, scrawny. They lived in the streets, in backyards, in the swamps of Becancour. Sam, Nydia, and Little Sam had never seen so many cats. The cats' eyes were glowing slits as they watched the newcomers. The town was ripe with evil. It seemed to waft in from the swamps with the hot, fetid breeze and breed in the minds of Becancour's citizens. Soon Sam, Nydia, and Little Sam would battle the forces of darkness. Standing alone against the ultimate predator—The Devil's Cat.

THE DEVIL'S HEART (2110, $3.95)

Now it was summer again in Whitfield. The town was peaceful, quiet, and unprepared for the atrocities to come. Eternal life, everlasting youth, an orgy that would span time—that was what the Lord of Darkness was promising the coven members in return for their pledge of love. The few who had fought against his hideous powers before, believed it could never happen again. Then the hot wind began to blow—as black as evil as The Devil's Heart.

THE DEVIL'S TOUCH (2111, $3.95)

Once the carnage begins, there's no time for anything but terror. Hollow-eyed, hungry corpses rise from unearthly tombs to gorge themselves on living flesh and spawn a new generation of restless Undead. The demons of Hell cavort with Satan's unholy disciples in blood-soaked rituals and fevered orgies. The Balons have faced the red, glowing eyes of the Master before, and they know what must be done. But there can be no salvation for those marked by The Devil's Touch.